The BOOK of MOM

The BOOK of MOM

A NOVEL

Taylor G. Wilshire

Nautilus Press

New York   Boston   London   Atlanta   San Diego

Published by Nautilus Press
Nautilus Press, a division of The Nautilus Works
For information contact: Nautilus Press P.O. Box 111
La Jolla CA, 92038 or visit us at www.thenautilusworks.com.

This novel is a work of fiction. Names, characters, places and incidents
are either the product of the author's imagination or are used ficti-
tiously, and any resemblance to actual persons, living or dead, business
establishments, events, or locales is entirely coincidental.

Special thanks to Archway & Mother's Circus for granting permission
to use their Animal Cookies.

Special thanks to the Foundation for A Course in Miracles for granting
permission to use excerpts from *A Course in Miracles.*

LIBRARY OF CONGRESS CATALOGING-IN- PUBLICATION DATA
Wilshire, Taylor.
The Book of Mom / Taylor Wilshire
1. Wilshire, Taylor—Fiction
2008900143

ISBN 978-0-9778018-1-7

Book design by Greg Smith

Printed in the United States of America.

A B C D

Special thanks to David Hough, Greg Smith, Victoria Austin-Smith, Carolyn Fox, Alex Jennings, Lisa Pumpkin, Rachel Myers, Jean Mefferd, Parker C. Arnold, Sunita L. Gupta, and S. Reasbeck.

This book is for my mother, who I wish could have met my children. But I know who watches over them in every moment of every day.

CHAPTER

One

"My mind is preoccupied with past thoughts."

I used to be a big-shot corporate executive. The real kind who gets the huge office, flies only first class, and makes an obscene amount of money. I was someone important, really important. Or at least I thought I was at the time.

That all changed when I gave birth to Alex, my first son, and thought what a ridiculous thing I used to do. What? Vice president of where? Who cares! I found the answer to life in a tiny, beautiful baby who melted my heart into liquid love. I loved being at home with my bundle of joy and just knew I'd be the most hands-on, attentive, amazing mom who ever existed. Not that being type-A had anything to do with it.

Parents magazine could have learned a few million things from me. For example, where were the articles on "I Know Best," I mean, "Mother Knows Best"? Or how to grow organic fruits and vegetables in your backyard and turn them into gourmet baby food delights that *Bon Appetit* would want to publish? Or how to use the number-one desktop publishing software to create the most artistic labels showing one's cherished cherub's face and handprints to personalize his storage containers, toys, clothes, snack holders, and backpacks? Missing. Totally missing—*Parents* magazine should have been calling me for some advice. Sure, parenting magazines had a few good tips now and then, but nothing like the 114 Web sites on child development and the two dozen books on parenting that I referenced religiously. Who said kids didn't come with manuals.

When Alex was three, I had Cole, my second cherub. Could a heart get even fuller?! I was in love times two. Who knew? Where were Socrates, Emerson, and Shakespeare on the meaning of love and life? The answer could clearly be found in my children.

Those were the blissful days of being busy doing all those wonderful mommy-and-me things like *Kinder Music, Water Babies* and *Tumbling-with-Me* classes, not to mention touring all the local museums and parks. I read an average of twenty books to each child per day—that is, after reading flash cards, giving baby massages and making musical instruments from toilet-paper rolls and dried macaroni. The things that we created were astonishing, amazing, mind-boggling: look out Einstein, Schubert, and Armstrong, two more coming!

It was all so perfect, flawless, and ideal until that *thing* happened—that horrible, heinous thing. That thing that no one warned me about, that no one talks or writes about—it came from nowhere. Okay, so maybe I might have heard someone whispering about it at the playground, but I never believed it could happen to *me*—the best mom in the universe. It was the collapse, breakdown, cave in, crumbling, disintegration and loss of me, or what I thought was me.

I had lost my mind, my body, and my spirit and was now left with a one-dimensional, dimwitted, off-course, dull and brainless over-doting monster. I mean mother.

I had no idea who I was anymore. Sure I knew my name and address and shoe size, but my brain began to shrivel at such an enormous rate that I couldn't find it anywhere. Somewhere between the diapers, lack of sleep, and Dr. Seuss, my passions, my interests, my wants and needs got lost. Sure I could tell you my kids' passions, wants and needs, and where everything that belonged to them was located. But not mine—gone, missing, vanished, dead.

For example, if I were to bump into Tony Robbins and he asked me out for a cup of coffee and said, "What are your passions—the things that excite, stimulate, and give you delight outside of your children?" I wouldn't be able to come up with anything. I would look at him as if he belonged to the planet Zefron and blurt, "But my children *are* my passions!"

Had I turned into an alien drone or an over-achieving mom? Was there a difference? Something happened after years of one-hundred-eleven-percent perfect mommism. I crashed.

There was no single event that caused the crash—no alien abduction or midnight lobotomy. It was more like a slow sucking of the brain, more like a morphine drip without the morphine—a brain drip. First, my kids stopped listening to me despite my daily scrutiny of my parenting library. There was no more magic in *1, 2, 3 Magic,* nor any logic in *Parenting with Love and Logic.* I needed a book titled *How to Feel Normal When You Feel So Stuck, Mad, and Pathetic!* Serving, serving, serving, serving meals, child safety, baths, games and love and laughter and rules sucked out most of my grey matter and left me with sludge.

And just when I thought two kids had taken all of my heart, intelligence, and wits, there was that overgrown third child—my husband, Blake. Yep, him, the guy who used to be such a manly man had become such a needy man—needing clean socks and clean underwear, needing a tidy house, needing dinner, needing his dry cleaning picked up, blah, blah, blah. I was afraid he was going to start asking for milk money when he left in the morning.

What the hell—had I turned into one of *those*? One of those women I feared and loathed when I was at work—a *Hausfrau*? You know, those women who bake cookies and brownies and send them off with the hubby to share with his pals in the break room. Martha Stewart, my mentor, could tell you what I am talking about. There I was, making art out of frosting, thinking it was the coolest thing until I realized what it truly was: an exercise in utter absurdity.

My husband tossed his thick mane of hair as he turned to me. "Hey, hon …" When I met Blake he was all blond, but now his hair, still in the same classic preppy cut, is adorned with grey. "Hey, honey, could you pick up some of those ice cream bars next time you're at the grocery store; you know, the ones with the nuts?" I rolled my eyes as I walked away. Now I had become his personal shopper.

There were moments when he did remember I had a brain outside of family services—after dinner, when the kids were finally tucked in bed and I had zero energy. That was when Blake needed and wanted to rehash his day at the office to get things off his chest. You know, brainstorm strategies or ideas he had been contemplating, or maybe be adored by his wife, who could have used some adoration coming her way. This neediness handicap came from wanting approval from his parents. He never got it. It's exhausting to adore someone who is so damn needy!

Blake was a corporate executive—he headed up the private counsel at a Fortune 100 company—and seemed to need a constant sounding board on difficult issues at work. I wanted to say to him, *Who cares about your damn meetings and those people in your office. I'm exhausted and no longer have a brain; can't you see the drip?* But it wouldn't matter even if I did. He would pay no attention and return to his acute non-listening skills—which are at the PhD level. That particular night, I wasn't even going to fake that I was interested. I was done, fried, crispy, and I was leaving his after-hours meeting. He was a mind-tapping, emotion-sucking organism wanting to make contact, and I was moving out of the kitchen fast. If I didn't bolt I would be talking about business crap all night long, and, frankly, I didn't give a shit about anyone else right then.

I was beat.

So as he talked and I ignored (pretending I was not ignoring by nodding my head and smiling), I opened the cabinet and reached for a moment that belonged to me. After filling my favorite green and blue ceramic mug with spring water and decaf mint green tea, I set it in the microwave. Looking over and acting engaged, I was really thinking about the book on my bedside table as he went on about a possible merger. And when the microwave beeped I gently excused myself from the non-paying advice, one-sided purge and sounding board summit and lied to him that I had to pee. With brewed tea in one hand, straightening and picking up my way through the house with the other, I finally made it to the bedroom, where I melted into a stack of pillows on the bed—a perfect nest. After pulling a soft down comforter to my waist, I let out the first breath of the day that belonged to me. The only breath I did not have to share, and before I could take my first sip of tea and read my first page, I was out, asleep.

My heart had stopped beating—was I the only one who knew? No, it wasn't cardiac arrest. It was life as a mom. I had forgotten what my heartbeat sounded like. Rushing from one thing to the next disassociated me from the sound of my own internal life force. Right now the force was sleeping, but it had only six and a half more hours before it would be woken up against its will, by grabbing, chubby hands.

Was I too far gone?

Yes.

CHAPT

Two

took drugs
someth
I
a

"*I am upset because I see a meaningless world.*"

I woke up the next morning in a funk. It wasn't the typical *I don't want to get out of bed because the covers are warm and the sky is still dark and the air is too cold* funk. Nor was it the type of funk that resisted the day-to-day mundane motions of getting dressed, fixing everyone breakfast, packing lunches and maybe brushing my teeth, if I could get to it—the usual weekday routine.

It was the *Oh shit I lost something* feeling that begged, *Could you tell me what the point is?* kind of funk. You know, the burning ache that asks, *You've got to be kidding—this is it?* I was stuck like glue in my own little depression—okay, maybe bigger than little. I didn't feel like I was enlightening the world with my wisdom. As a matter of fact, I had no wisdom; I was being weighed down by my own spiritual strife and lack of awareness. Was there a drug that could get me out of this? I knew a mom who

, and she was always happy. Maybe she was onto
ng.

slumped out of bed, pushed my feet into my slippers,
d dribbled my way through the morning, yelling only
once at my older son and feeling horrible for doing it—even
though he was squishing my younger son and giving him a
noogie, wasn't dressed for school, and hadn't taken a bite
of his breakfast or listened to a single word I had said since
he had woken up.

My children's screeches, running feet, and regular loud
and exultant sounds made it impossible to have one mil-
limoment of silence. Not even *one* gap in the noise to have
one solid thought to myself. Not even an undersized instant
of peace or one itty-bitty breath that belonged to just me. It
was Wednesday morning, and the biggest penis of the house
had already left for his weekly early-morning meeting.

I wanted a stretch of uninhabited land, far away, where
I could rest surrounded by glowing candles and burning
incense on an overstuffed, pillowed bed with angels fanning
me with palm fronds. I wanted solace, or at least chanting
monks, that reminded me of all the things to be grateful for.
I wanted divine intervention.

God must have been busy or had better people to work
on—someone with at least a drop of hope. I couldn't think
of one positive thought or one affirmation to reprogram my
thinking to something cheerful. No metaphysical mantras,
no yoga positions, no world peace prayers would come to
me. Just lethargic motions of a day going by.

It's not that I was yearning for my old life in the office,
or even wanting a different day-to-day routine. I wanted a
piece of *me* back, the piece that felt satiated in life and ful-
filled to the rim. But even more importantly, I wanted a little
respect, a little adoration, at least some acknowledgment of

8

my life and what I was doing. More than just a peck on the cheek and a *bye* from my husband, who didn't even look me in the eye before he left for his day of full sentences, intellectual stimulation, and normal brain activity.

I needed confirmation that this was my best and final legacy. I wanted the skies to part, revealing a thunderbolt or some other sign from God to show me, "Yep, this is your purpose, your destiny. It's exactly what I had in mind." However, there was no burning bush or whispering angel; just the hum of the dishwasher.

So what does a stay-at-home mom, slightly out of shape—okay, maybe more than slightly—with uncombed brown shoulder-length hair pulled back in a scrunchie, unbrushed teeth, near-sighted blue eyes with day-old mascara smudge, dressed in sweats with a patch of oatmeal on the left shoulder, do when she is not feeling spiritually awake? Drop the older child at kindergarten and get on with the day, of course.

My sole regret is that I did not at least gargle, change my top, or wash my face, because that was the day I dropped off my child at the exact moment the fabulous beautiful moms were dropping off their offspring.

"Oh, hi," they say, taunting me with their perfectly glossed lips, exquisitely plucked brows, and shoes bought someplace other than Marshall's. These are the moms who have *careers*, some because they have to, and some because they have to feel important, though they can afford to stay at home.

"What have you been up to?" They smell so good, showered and perfumed.

Instead of saying, *Oh, the usual. Changing eighty diapers a day, doing a million loads of laundry, cleaning toilets, making bite-sized meals, folding laundry, playing with building blocks, and reading parenting Web sites and picture books 'til I drop,* I say, "Still consulting and working at home." A complete load of crap—the last time I even talked to one of my clients was a year ago, and that was to e-mail the latest pictures of the kids.

"Oh, you're *consulting,*" as if they are saying, *Oh really—you might be hello worthy. I didn't know you had a real life. Maybe you're someone worth talking to …if only you didn't look so bad.* But they were too busy to talk. So we didn't. We got into our separate sucking-out-the-ozone SUVs and went our merry ways … with one small exception. I didn't feel merry; I felt worse. I lied. Not to them as much as to myself. I cheated myself of my own self-worth, but even worse, I cheated my kids; I devalued them. In that lie, I denied them of their worth and my own existence. Now on top of feeling out of sync and in a funk, I was a heinous villain—a horrible, unloving mother.

So I half-heartedly worked out, showered, brushed my hair, changed into a nice outfit, and put makeup on, but there was no one to see me when I was done. No one to think, *Oh, she looks nice today.* It was too late; they were already off to their day with visions of shlump-mom in their well-kempt heads.

The day moves too slowly when I'm playing with Cole on the floor. I think of the people I left behind in my corporate world. Would they be interested that my gorgeous angel is now walking and talking, or more interested in the corner office with the breathtaking view that is now theirs?

I did go back to work after the birth of my first son, breast pump under one arm, laptop, briefcase and Starbucks in the other. After I set up the baby pictures on my desk and reset my voicemail, one of my direct-reports walked in.

"So, what's the latest?" he asked in a professional and casual tone.

I knew something was amiss when he seemed uninterested in my four-hundred-page baby scrapbook. Was it the sonogram pictures that turned him off or the pictures of me breast- feeding? One will never know. I think he was asking, *What's the latest in the company and how does it impact me?*—not what the latest miracle in my life was. My perception of corporate life was forever changed. I was no longer the pit bull with the velvet glove. I was milk-leaker in the stained suit, skirt fastened in the back by a safety pin to accommodate my postpartum baby fat.

I didn't last long in my old job as vice president in a multibillion-dollar corporation. My grey matter had turned into sludge from hormones that stole my photographic memory. I became soft. I became nice. The overdrive turned into peddling.

The company didn't get rid of me; I got rid of myself. The guilt of leaving my baby with someone who could never love him the way I did drove me to take an exit package. It wasn't that I couldn't still make the numbers or bring in the revenue, it just didn't matter to me the way it used to. It wasn't important anymore.

CHAPTER

Three

"I am determined to see things differently."

I am looking outside the kitchen window to the bruised grass where the kids played that morning. I am still thinking about their dirty bare feet when I call Katie. My life had more than its first stroke of luck when I met my best friend in college. She has been my sanity channel for the last twenty years.

When I saw Katherine Elizabeth Wilson walk out the doors of the student union, I thought I knew her from somewhere. We stared at each other a little too long, stopped, and said almost at the same time, "Do I know you? Where do I know you from?" We looked hard and long, but the truth is, that was the first time we had met. She thought it was an old soul thing. I didn't know what it was except weird and somehow familiar.

Katie was that natural beauty that all guys wanted to date not because of her hot body or her ideal blond hair—

the kind people pay a lot of money for—or her warm brown eyes that would make a wide-eyed doe ask, *Are we related?* Guys lined up because she didn't think she was beautiful. She was striking, smart and funny, the perfect mix of cool, yet she never knew it.

Katie could watch people without getting in their space—really observe them. She took people in and easily made them feel comfortable. It was her openness and modest confidence that drew people to her.

Even though all the guys loved her and wanted to be her boyfriend, she had other things on her mind. Horses. Just like me, her first love had four legs and the good barn smell. She was a year older than I was, but she might as well have been ten thousand years older. She went about her life slowly and smoothly like her backhand in tennis, so flawless I would just watch in awe as she made a perfect point against me. It was the only time it was okay to lose a point because she was poetry in motion. There wasn't anything she couldn't do. But try convincing her of that.

Forget it.

No matter how many times I told her how amazing she was, no matter how many times I pointed out all the million things she could do better than anyone on the entire planet. Forget about it. She never got it and still doesn't. She's like someone in a Greek myth—a goddess trapped in human form.

The difference between Katie and me is that Katie can do everything but thinks she can't, and I can't do much but think I can do everything. Too much self-confidence can backfire and often does, but that still doesn't stop me. I only wish I had her talent to back up my ego.

But the difference between us goes beyond that. For instance, the only reason I beat Katie at tennis time after time is not that I'm a better player than she is—not even close. It's because she's not competitive enough to care. I care. I care a lot and love beating her every time, because I know that she is better than me. I love squashing her like a bug and then announcing to the world what I have just done. I'm not modest or humble, I'm a pain in the ass and she just laughs at me. Don't get me wrong, she doesn't always laugh. She gets pissed that I play with her head more than I play the game. But that's what we do on and off the courts, and for some strange reason it works, we work. We make each other better because our strengths and weaknesses are the exact opposite, and somehow we magically fit.

I know and have always known that I've gotten the better end of the stick—she's more patient than I am, less judgmental, more loving, and just all around saint-perfect. The thing is, I'm too selfish to let her go to the people she deserves. She's let me be her best friend for more than twenty years, and I'm thankful and grateful that she has held on, because she has made my life so much better.

"I gotta see you," I say, walking with the cordless wedged between my ear and shoulder. My head is stuck in the kitchen cabinet as I try to pack the diaper bag—bottles, water, lunch containers filled with Cheerios, cut-up grapes, paper towels, baby wipes, small toys, and chunky books that fit in the palm of my hand.

"Sure. You wanna come up or should I come down?" she says in her sultry voice. You could swear she worked for 1-900-HOT-BABE. It's from too many cigarettes in college, an indulgence she gave up when she met her husband. She'd do anything for him; she says that love does that.

"I'm coming up. I have to see you ...You were right," I say.

"About what?"

"About balancing my life. I am so off kilter I can't see straight."

Katie lives in Orange County and we live in San Diego, but she and I aren't natives to California. Katie and I are New Yorkers.

She dragged me out to California against my will. First to help her get settled into her apartment when she landed her first job after college, and then to offer me space in her home when I landed my second job. She did everything first, like turning forty before I did, having kids, and becoming spiritually enlightened. I was hoping she would screw up first and then I could learn from her mistakes. The problem was that I was the one making all the mistakes and wrong judgments; she always got it right while I was still upside down.

"How do you get balanced when you feel so wobbly?" I ask.

"One step at a time," she responds calmly.

"Yeah, yeah, yeah. No, I'm serious."

"Okay, first you need to find your breath."

"What's wrong with you? I know how to breathe. I'm feeling depressed!"

"I hear you, but when you slow down and listen to your breath, things shift. It's a small thing but powerful. It takes you to the divine."

"What the hell have you been smoking? I need real advice—I have no clue who I am anymore."

"Of course you do," she says flatly.

"I think I'd know!"

"Well, we'll start with what you *do* know when I see you."

So, I drove up, along I-5, to her home. She would have toys on the kitchen floor set out for Cole, toys that her own kids stopped playing with years ago—a toddler scooter or a box of fat Legos. We'd have only an hour and a half before I'd have to drive back in order to miss traffic and pick up Alex.

We sat in her backyard—roomy and elegant compared to our teeny-tiny space. Our yard is large enough for the boys to do doughnuts around the patio furniture with their bikes, but not large enough to hit a baseball or put in a pool—big enough to just about breathe in a small breath. In Katie's yard, you could really inhale.

"What happened to me?" I say as I set Cole down on a patch of grass; he heads straight for a tiny trike.

"Tate, you're perfect."

"No, I'm serious."

"You put everything into the kids and didn't save anything for you. It happens when your kids are small."

"How come you're so perfect?" I ask, looking at her nicely matching outfit.

She laughs her laugh, head thrown back, that ideal blond hair swinging from right to left, eyes closed. "Oh God, I'm not."

"But I know you—you're so balanced."

"Maybe at times and it's only because I practice—a lot!" she says as she pours tea out of a porcelain teapot that belonged to her grandmother. She is as graceful as a geisha; I am mesmerized by her movements and wonder when she's going to pull out the fans and start dancing.

"I know, I know, yoga, meditation. Blah, blah, blah."

"You're the best mom, you should be so proud of yourself," she says sincerely.

"Yes, they are cute! Yes, I love them … Could I please have a life now?"

"I thought you'd never ask." Cole is now off the trike and gently touching a bright yellow daisy. He touches the petals so tenderly, unlike his older brother at that age. Alex would have torn off the heads and pulled out the other flowers by their roots. Cole looks over and gives me an open smile through his soft chubby cheeks—his large blue eyes swallow me whole.

"How do you get help when you don't know how to get help and don't want to burden your best friend?" I ask.

"You're not burdening me." Her face is soft and open. "But I do wish I could give better advice—and feel like I'm really helping you."

"You think I need a shrink?"

"No, I'm not saying that—but it helped me—and on some level, I think everyone could use professional help."

"God, am I that bad?"

"Would you stop—I'm talking about me."

I am momentarily stunned at the notion that my perfect friend needed even one 50-minute couch session to work through her issues. "Maybe you're right," I barely whisper.

"Oh come on, lighten up. We're just talking. Do you realize you haven't changed a bit since the days we used to run around in college?"

"God, that's depressing."

"No, silly, you look exactly the same. Same size-six body she knows I'm bordering on double digits). Classic face, amazing chocolate hair and blue eyes. Killer combo. And you still look twenty-five, not one wrinkle. How do you do that? How do you keep your enthusiasm and energy that's so contagious? Intelligent beyond words and just plain timeless. I love everything about you, even your goofiness—your quirks are good, too."

"What do you mean?" I ask. I know she is doing a bad job of changing the subject, but I have no problem taking the compliments.

"Fear of nose hairs."

"Yeah, thank God for trimmers." She isn't even funny, but I laugh anyway.

"How many do you have? Heh, heh, heh?" Katie asks in her trademark sarcastic three-syllable laugh.

Then she turns serious again. "You have the ability to stretch yourself and push yourself ..." She's trying to cover, to butter me up because she knows that I am a lost cause.

I'm no longer buying the act. "Where are you going with this?"

"Tate, it's clear to me that you possess natural spirituality ... What I know most about you is that you are a spiritual master."

Katie must be fasting and delirious. She knows me, but now she's spouting fiction.

She is right about my liking all forms of philosophy, but I'm definitely not feeling spiritual—at all. Master, maybe; of bullshit, quite possibly.

"In college, you loved an intellectual conversation and hated jocks even though you became one." *From my fear of getting fat,* I think. "Remember how much you liked Kierkegaard and liked quoting the great thinkers?"

"Like I can remember anything these days?"

She forgot to add my rebellion from organized religion, especially Episcopalianism—which we were raised in. Our journeys were never the same when it came to spirituality, which made me wonder how we really had stayed friends this long with so little in common. She was freshening up our cups of ginger tea from the warm teapot, replacing the old lemon slices with new ones. I was craving her iced tea, the one she makes with the perfect ice cubes that have frozen sprigs of mint inside.

Katie adds, "... So I think you've stayed so beautiful because you're willing to open yourself and be vulnerable."

"Don't you think you're confusing me with yourself?" I counter as she sips her tea, swirling the lemon and watching it sink.

"No."

With a half grin I ask, "Are you looking to borrow something, are you in trouble, you need a little cash?"

"Funny."

CHAPTER
Four

"There is nothing to fear."

Katie had suggested it, and I went after it. I researched a good shrink like nobody's business. I asked friends if they knew anyone, asked my doctor, asked my kids' pediatrician. I read *Psychology Today,* which suggested ways to find a good one and how to make sure they qualify. I wanted a cognitive therapist; someone who wouldn't make me re-live my life—birth to present day—and go over and over my problems with my parents. In other words, I wanted to move forward, not backward into a neurosis-obsessing adult child.

I searched online, I searched the phone book, but I ended up using a less strategic approach: I found my shrink at the gym. No, she wasn't working out with me in an aerobics class, nor peddling on a stationary bike next to mine. My new shrink was the one I heard two ladies talking about in the locker room; they made her sound like a magician. Two glowing references were better than shopping through the physicians directory.

On the way over to her office, I rehearsed in my head how the first appointment would go. I would be calm and look normal and not go into my past, or interrupt her or ask her a million questions. I would let her direct the flow of the session. I would be sane.

Her office was in a basic and almost generic office park. The lobby was not high-end or low-end, with a fountain in the courtyard that probably came from Home Depot. The floors were ceramic tile, not marble. The white walls featured no fine art, just pictures bought at Target or K-Mart. The general atmosphere was not tasteless, just mildly tacky.

The doctor directed me with her hand to a comfy beige chair opposite another comfy chair with three throw pillows that I had seen at TJ Maxx—floral with tassels. I sat, nervous but trying not to be nervous.

Right after she introduced herself, she had me close my eyes and take a breath. A deep, slow, long breath and then another and then another until I felt calm. I mean calmer: I was still nervous and feared that she would sense how needy I was, or that I was weak, insane or maybe a bit like a freak. I dreaded she would prescribe meds—Prozac, Xanax or the latest tranquilizer—on our first visit, which might not have been such a bad idea. I took a total of seven breaths, slower and slower, until I felt light-headed and relaxed.

Her first question is, "What brings you here?"

And then, without warning, the nonstop chatter came rolling out of my mouth. My speech was too fast and relentless. I expressed every thought from birth to that day—a data-dump stuck on send-mode gone bad. I started with my mother.

21

"If you had met my mother you would have loved her. Everyone did." My mother was stunningly beautiful, with blue eyes that pierced the sky. She enveloped everyone in her warm heart and nurturing love. She wasn't the touchy-feely type who drools all over you. She was the kind, approachable type who you are in awe of but not intimidated by. I'm not looking into my therapist's eyes because she might want to change the subject and I wanted to talk—a lot.

"She was not of this place, you know; she was from a place that doesn't exist here, because she was that good—too good. I'm not just bragging because she was my mother; I am stating the fact that everyone knew." Now I do look into her eyes, and her head bobs up and down like she agrees with what I am saying even though she has never met my mom. I notice that she has tucked her light-brown hair behind her ear and crossed her legs like mine.

"I wasn't in love with her heart as much as I was in love with her mind." She had a mind and memory that would stop the great seers in their tracks. She wasn't haughty or in-your-face about her intellect; she was gentle and kind with her information, offering it to you like a piece of her famous cinnamon raisin bread which she made from scratch. She'd cut it into thick chunky pieces and cover them in butter that would melt and ooze—it tasted like heaven. "It wasn't just that she was talented at everything; it was her deep gratitude and enthusiasm for life that were so contagious." I've gone off in my head like the therapist is no longer in the room.

"I wanted my children to know her and feel her love embrace them, feel her warmth, know her unlimited depth of forgiveness and kindness. She died two weeks before my first son was born." She was riding her bike, enjoying the sunshine, before a stroke hit her head-on. She died three

THE BOOK OF MOM

days later. "I was pregnant and ready to pop. I couldn't get on a plane to New York." I didn't get to see her in the hospital before she slipped away to the place where she was from. This marked the spot where my brothers, father and I started to crumble.

"What really sucked was that I was unable to be there at the funeral service to say a last goodbye and make sure she was really dead. To this day I wonder if she really has left us at all. I miss her. I miss the way she smelled and her voice and her wit and her hugs that lasted forever."

She hasn't gone far, she radiates through my heart and creeps out of me every time I bite my tongue before I want to swear out loud. Or when I hug or goof around with my kids. Somewhere along the way I became her, not all of her, just parts of her—some good and some not so good.

I was crying like I always am when I talk about my mother—which is never. So I guess I was crying for the first time.

CHAPTER
Five

"My happiness and my function are one."

I have just finished cleaning up the morning dishes, wiped off the countertops, fed the cat, cleaned off Cole's face with a napkin, and set out a cardboard tube of Tinker Toys. I am about to sit on the floor to see what kind of tower I can build before Cole decides to crash it. I really do not want to be building this—quick, someone give me a hit of acid to make this fun.

But somehow my body relaxes as Cole picks up the next orange spoke and puts it in a round wooden center and begins to build on his own, without making a mess. I let out a slow breath as my eyes wander outside through the kitchen window to the backyard. The backyard is small but lush: Tall palm trees and a perfectly manicured, tiny lawn bordered by flowering bushes and shrubbery. The plants in the flower beds are positioned flawlessly according to the landscape architect's vision and maintained to perfection.

That's Blake for you. Everything that Blake touches is aesthetically pleasing, everything that he oversees or manages reflects his attention to detail.

Blake gets that from his mom—the woman who likes to clean. Who has heard of such a thing? She cleans her house obsessively, but what she really wants to clean up is the mess of her life—her husband's never-ending drinking, and her inability to forgive him or her past. And this cleaning obsession rubbed off on Blake. He cleans too and has inherited his mom's perfectionism. The apple doesn't fall far from the tree.

My eyes rest softly on the fountain set in the right corner of the yard under the palm trees. As I watch the water pop and flow from one tier to the next, I am hypnotized by the sight and the tranquil sound. My mind carries me back to one of the days in college when Katie would sketch pictures of me. On the bottom of these pictures she would add long, detailed descriptions of what she had drawn, as if the viewer were blind:

Tate. Her nose is aristocratic and matches her chin within an oval face, piercing blue eyes like her mother's, and her straight hair is often pulled back with a tortoise-shell hair band. In the winter she wears leather riding gloves when she drives her car to remind her that she rode a large bay gelding over fences. She's got thin wrists and thin ankles and holds weight, if she does hold weight, in her hips.

There was one of me looking out the dorm window:

Tate. Taken by model agency for Ralph Lauren. Her parents would have killed her if they found this and would have told her, "You are only to be in the public eye on your birth announcement, wedding announcements, and obituary." She asked the agency if they would pay in clothes versus check; they declined and so did she.

Another one of Katie's practical jokes. I was never approached by Ralph Lauren, but my parents would have said something like that. She always made me look better than I was.

I miss her. I pick up the phone.

"God, I wish I could see you every day," I say when she answers.

"I know, we live too far—and have kids."

"Why is it so hard to be normal?"

"This is the new normal," she sighs.

"Oh God, that's so depressing. Could you just talk to me and tell me your profound journey, because I'm not getting it." I sound too needy, but instead of hanging up she feels my heart, and unfolds herself.

"You know, I didn't come into this amazing crazy world of motherhood looking for a spiritual truth. I just wanted to see my kids grow—be the one who taught them about the world. I definitely wasn't prepared for what I got! You know, I *do* remember what it was like to operate on no sleep and maybe a shower a week. No one craved a pat on the back or a 'Hey, job well done' more than me. But then something happened. Over the years the interests that I had in college, like Buddhism, resurfaced. You know all this, I know, but I've got to tell you again to remind you that sometimes things take time. I knew I had to find my deeper sense of purpose, and the search was actually the reward."

"I feel so pathetic," I say as I give Cole banana slices.

"You know, when my kids were small like yours, I had the same feelings, like needing a sense of contribution that comes from a paycheck. Don't forget, I made more money than Jack."

"Me too."

"I felt my creativity was squashed from full-time parenting my young children; that's not to say I didn't love them, love being with them, cherish them and know it's a privilege to be a stay-at-home mom. But it's a lot to ask from someone to be so selfless. What never changed was the possibility to feel my oneness with something bigger than me. But when I finally did try to meditate or quiet my mind and sit down and have that still moment that belonged to me, I'd fall asleep. And the few times where I didn't fall asleep, I was thinking of the laundry, or paying bills, or getting my grocery list going—the myriad of motherhood and mundane household stuff. I know how you feel, because I felt it too. The only difference is that I've had more time to be persistent and work on me—and my kids are older. I looked for answers from great Zen masters of yoga, from the pastor at church, and in all my books on self-help and theology, and then I found the answers in my own kids. All the things I do right and wrong get mirrored right back to me every day. They are the best teachers on what I have to keep working on, and with them I *have* to be present in the moment. The best thing I know about motherhood is that I don't know anything. I'm constantly learning."

"God, I wish I were you ..."

"Wherever you go, you are there. Pay attention. Don't just eat, and read, and sleep. Look around and observe. The only time I've found that I can really observe is when I slow down, and the only way I can slow down is to meditate more, do yoga, and breathe. Lots of deep breaths—like when I want to scream, like when I want to run away, like when I just want one more minute to myself ... I breathe, and slowly my breath comes back to me and I can get through. What I've learned is that it's like a plane getting ready to crash: the oxygen mask goes on *me* first so that I can help my kids put on theirs."

"Okay, now I really have to see you," I say in desperation.

"Come on up."

"Really?"

"I just got back from yoga and was gonna take a shower. By the time you get here, I'll be done with the stuff I have to do. Okay, let's see ... we'll have two hours before you have to go back to San Diego."

"Cool."

It's a fifty-minute drive without traffic and worth every second. The words to *Buzz, Buzz, Buzz Goes the Bee* are tolerable after the eighth time because I know that I will be getting to see my best friend and obtain some free therapy. Luckily, Cole likes the car—as long as there are continuous *Wee Sings* and snacks and picture books and the secret stash of lollipops. I love when he is strapped into his car seat, not out of my sight and safe. Driving north on the 5 in my mobile glass bubble, I can't help but enjoy the scenery, the ocean to my left—endless.

California. A desert with a lot of sprinklers that make things stay green all the time. The state where palm trees and bougainvillea feel completely at home. The land smells like eucalyptus and ocean breezes. And sand—there's lots of sand: at the beaches, at play grounds, and yes, of course, in the uncovered desert where no sprinklers live.

The homes. Nouveau Spanish architecture is the norm. Tract houses that are trying to look original and never do. Stucco upon stucco. Tile upon tile. Dry.

There is all this ocean, but by no means do you ever see a starfish. Unlike the East Coast, where there are so many pockets of land unspoiled by time, this land is spoiled rotten. Too much new, too little old. Old was built in 1950—go figure.

Don't get me wrong. There's nothing bad about continuous clear sunshine and perfectly mild days. The problem is, there's no room for depression, a necessity for a New Yorker who is used to overcast, gloomy weather—the backdrop for sadness.

I think I'd go mad without a best friend. No, I *would* be mad without a best friend. My mind would race endlessly and obsess on everything that I'd say and do. Like the stupid things that I say, when I talk too much and people don't get that I'm joking, or they just don't get me and I feel so alone and so awkward. If I didn't have a best friend, all I would do is obsess endlessly about having one. I'd feel constant loneliness and desolation, my days would be vacant. My nonstop neurotic thoughts and slipping self-esteem would make my heart ache, no, break into tiny pieces.

And then there would be the incessant search for someone to be a best friend candidate, someone I could call three or four times a day to talk with about nothing and everything. God, maybe I'm co-dependent. I think I *am* co-dependent—that will be the first thing I ask Katie when I see her.

"Do you think I'm co-dependent?"

"You know, if I didn't know you, I wouldn't know you."

She smiles and her top lip disappears.

"What's that supposed to mean?"

"You would never ask a stupid question like that!"

"Oh God, so I am?"

"Honey, you need some rest. Come on back."

She takes us to her kitchen that should be in Provence. The warm walls are painted a mix of creamy beige and muted yellow. Accents of white and Oriental blue are everywhere—from the plates that hang on the walls to the valances over the kitchen window. The custom cabinets have an old-world feel of golden brown wood, and over the center island there is a pot rack filled with old and new copper pots, all heavily used.

What I love most about the kitchen is the granite countertops: the deep greens and amber chunks and wisps of cocoa, and what makes them really remarkable, a root-like amethyst veining. I see something different every time I look at them. My countertops are white marble and ideal for baking, the only thing I'm good at in the kitchen. Hers have big personality, whereas mine say *quiet please*—they are the opposite of each of us.

If you asked Katie what her favorite thing in the kitchen is, she would say it's the copper country sink with the perfect, clean lines of its simple faucet. She pays no attention to the dark, wide-planked hardwood floors, or to her pantry, which is a mile deep and a mile wide. You'd think she'd love the window over the sink that overlooks the backyard, or the oversize Viking stove, or the breakfast table brought over from Europe with its country benches. Nope, she loves that sink, not because it's gorgeous but because "it's about the water, the sound, the feel."

Of course, Katie doesn't even need such an extravagant kitchen; she could make her gourmet delights on a wood-burning pit outside.

Her cuisine of choice is rustic-gourmet: breads and tortes filled with cheeses that cost a fortune, and countless French meat dishes with sauces that take all day to make and melt in your mouth shortly after reaching your lips. My favorites are her grilled meat paradises and salads made from the freshest organic produce, blue cheeses, apples, roasted hazelnuts ... And her homemade soups and lemon squares. Stay away from her lemon squares—deadly.

When she is in the kitchen, she is always cooking. It

calms her, it relaxes her, and her gift is for the rest of us to enjoy. Her whole house has that comfortable and generous spirit. Nothing says *Sit on me carefully*; everything calls *Sink into me and relax.*

Everything is meant to be handled, felt, and stroked. Like the small beach stones in a cup, the Italian silk curtains, the French damask throw pillows. And her remarkable sense of color: it's not over the top, it's just right. "Every home should have a bit of red, and lettuce green, and robin's-egg blue." Her house is an extension of her soul.

My style tends to be more cottage and new traditional, sprinkled with what I grew up with, from hunting pictures to duck decoys. The tones are muted and subtle, to calm my personality. And every light is on a dimmer. The dimmers are Blake's idea. He thinks all lights should be turned down a notch; maybe he feels the same about me.

"Blake is driving me crazy," I say, eating one of the fish crackers she has put out for Cole in a plastic bowl.

"Husbands do that." She places some blanched veggies and dip right in front of me.

"He's working too much." I take some broccoli and lightly tap it into the dip.

"Work is part of their identity."

"We're not having sex."

Her eyebrows rise, but she doesn't say a word.

"Okay, so maybe I'm part of the problem—I'm just so tired."

She still says nothing. She has sex all the time in every position.

"Okay, I'm not interested."

"Well, if you want to change that, just go to bed naked." And I'm thinking, *Why would I want to do that? She doesn't get it. I don't want to have sex with* him.

"My marriage is not so perfect," I say instead.

"And whose is?"

"Yours."

"Ha!"

"No, I'm serious."

CHAPTER
Six

"My grievances hide the light of the world in me."

My marriage used to be perfect. Blake used to be my soul mate. He used to get me and love me unconditionally. That changed when his form of communication turned into, "Can you say whatever you have to say during a commercial?"

The only things outside of work that were ever on his mind were sex and power tools. I used to think all the things that we loved about each other were what we lacked in ourselves. That put us in a place of continuous growth, making us better people. Depending on your definition of better. He used to surprise me with his kind heart and generous nature. Now he just surprises me with how self-consumed he is. The days of praise and acknowledgment are gone. Now it's just a constant string of demands. Marriage can do that.

I had become the thing that I hated in other women:

a male basher, male stereotyper, and male labeler. I didn't want to tell Katie it had come to this. She wouldn't get it. But maybe she would. I give it a try.

"Sex isn't so good anymore."

"Really?"

"It used to be a day of Twister or connect-the-dots. Now it's just the same old pin-the-tail on-the-donkey without the blindfold; one move and it's over. What happened to lust and passion? Blake's got no sense of time and place in the heat of the moment?"

"Have you told him?"

"He doesn't think anything is wrong."

I can't tell Katie too much for fear of judgment. She wouldn't understand a dry spell, they don't exist for her.

In my life, a month passes and Blake will realize, *I ain't been getting any.* So he does his typical thoughtful and loving move, the well-thought-out plan, the Casanova strategy of greatness: he grabs his balls and asks, "You wanna do it?" With that romantic euphemism, I am entranced—not. Men. They need to stop asking and just charge, like a bull to the red cape.

So I go about my mindless duties of making dinner, caring for the kids, and the thousand endless and tiresome tasks that come with running a household, and then finally get the bath that I've wanted all day, slip into bed with a good book, and then there *he* is.

Not even, *Hey, what are you reading?* or *How was your day?* I look over at the clock; it is 8:47. Then there it is— squeeze right breast, squeeze left, and then the pineapple is taken over, pump, pump, and then he is dead weight on top of me.

"God, that was great," he says in a raspy voice, sweat on his brow.

I look over at the clock; it is 8:59. Then he says, "Wow! Why don't we do this more often?" And I'm thinking to myself, *Are you serious?*

Unbelievably, his next words are, "Man, how long were we doing that—almost an hour?" And he *really* means it! I say, "Oh, yeah, at least." He rolls over and starts snoring, and I'm thinking, *Is this it?* And the sad fact is, he thought he was King Kong Dong on his last parade, a marathon Casanova, and I'm thinking, *So this is marriage?*

Katie's marriage, on the other hand, is perfect. Not that I'm comparing. When Katie first met her husband, Jack Welks, in grad school, it was more than love at first sight, it was a sacred contract. One of the first things she said to me when she was falling in love with him was, "I can't believe how much my family is going to love him!" They're two Anglo-Saxons from the same Bostonian pod. Their ancestral roots run deep into the blue-blood soil. Katie is elegance with a Bohemian twist, and he is intellectual WASP—someone who recites Latin not to show you that he knows it, but because it is part of his normal speech. She's the only one who understands it. I always hope he'll utter something I know, like *carpe diem*, but that never happens, so I always feel stupid in his presence. But when he smiles, which is rarely, the game is over. His beauty radiates from within, his essence reveals itself, and it will knock you out—knock you out cold.

Our husbands are opposites, like Katie and I. Jack loves a game of squash or golf. He played rugby in college and likes anything to do with a pack. He's an intellectual who likes to play with other boys. He must have had a lot of playdates as a kid.

Blake likes solitude. His sport of choice has nothing to do with rubbing bodies or bouncing balls, it has all to do with the space between him and the trail. His recreation is running. His mantra is, "I run, therefore I am." It's not that he can't do all the other WASP sports that Jack does; he can and is really good at them. But that doesn't concern him. It's not about the glory, it's about the stillness. It's about the quiet. Running is Blake's moving meditation; it's where he makes things happen, where he manifests the miracles in his life. It's where he returns to center.

When I first met Blake I thought, *Nope, not my type.* We were in the workforce, high up on our corporate ladders. I was dating BMOC types. Physically Blake fit the frat-boy mold: clean cut, classic, blond, blue-eyed, but he was different—aloof, not showy. He didn't have the charismatic bad-boy charm I was used to; he was more of a loner. I later found out that he was just shy and a big advocate of personal space. The other thing about Blake is his height— 5'9½". He calls himself a medium man, but the truth is, he's short; short in my book, short in many women's books. What woman doesn't love a tall man? But the fact is, all the tall ones get taken first and fast. It's the short and medium men that you choose from when you put your career first.

Blake looked like a prep-school type, but he went to public schools. His parents were lower middle class and didn't earn enough to put him through college, so he went on full scholarship to Northwestern. He became a lawyer despite the fact that even though he got into Harvard and Yale, his father thought lawyers were one step below the anti-Christ. Blake danced to the beat of his own drum and didn't do things to impress others, not even his parents. He was all about fulfilling himself. It was that very trait that made me fall in love with him and fall hard. That same trait bit me in the ass after we were married.

I used to think Blake had other admirable qualities as

well. He surrounds himself with people more accomplished than he is—so that he pushes himself beyond what he thinks he is capable of. For example, if he were to run with anyone, he would choose a semi-pro-marathoner type. He once said he married me because I was more sensitive and more emotionally complex; he said he knew he would stretch. Bunch of crap.

Like Katie, Blake has always been an observer of people. The difference is, he watches them and, *I* think, categorizes them too. He can tell the type of person you are by the company you keep, by the words you use, by the way you move. When we were dating, he had the habit of staring off into space, with a look of silent benevolence. When I asked him what he was thinking, I was fully prepared for the male truth: "I was checking out the girl's boobs at that table," or "Nothing, just zoning," but instead I'd get answers like, "Do you think love is a soul thing or a chemical thing?" "Do you think that people are wired differently or do they just use less of what we all have?" "Huh?" was always my response. I stopped asking because I was sure his next answer would be, "I was thinking about the urinal cake in the bathroom and wondering if you could tell by the DNA what type of personality peed on it?"

Other guys would label him "a good guy." He will replace the bottle on the office water cooler when it's empty, and he'll do it when no one is looking to avoid drawing attention to his good deed. He will always pick up the check when we have company, also when no one is looking. But even though he's sensitive, he's human—male-human. His e-mails are no longer than five syllables. He still scratches his balls when he watches television, and says, "What?" like, *Come on, they itch,* and he reads a magazine when he "takes a dump."

It's a given that he still likes to listen to NPR and watch the History, Discovery and PBS channels. After all these years, he still hasn't changed his shape: he still isn't six feet tall, and he is the exact same weight he was in college. The color of his eyes hasn't changed; neither has his smile. To tell you the truth, the only thing that's changed is that he's more of what he was before; softer toward children, more introspective, more successful, and more at peace with himself—or so I thought.

The difference between men and women is this: at 3:30 in the morning, when the two- year-old is crying and coughing, the wife pushes the man out of bed to go check on the child because she has gone in the five nights before. When the man goes in, he pats the kid's head and walks out of the room with the child still crying and almost choking on his own phlegm. The man proceeds to go to the bathroom to relieve himself and then walks into the kitchen to take a Tylenol. He goes back to the little boy's room ten minutes later. The child is still coughing, crying, and having a hard time breathing because he is so congested. The man pats the boy's head again and then proceeds to go to sleep in the little boy's bed, thinking that his manly presence alone will quiet him as he squishes the small body against the wall.

The child is still coughing and crying ten minutes later. When the mother walks in, the father is asleep, snoring, and the boy is now drenched in urine. "Blake, he's soaked! Did you check him or give him anything for his cough?" The father answers, "Whaaaht!" Like, *What did I do wrong?* He sees no problem with the situation. Everything is taken care of in his eyes, so he thinks, *Why are you waking me up?* The mother changes the child, gives him some medicine, rubs his back, and puts him back next to the father, who hasn't moved an inch from the child's bed and is now snoring at top decibels. Why is it that the earth can revolve around men and somehow they can get away with it? Oh, that's right—because we let them.

Loving someone is easy when things are easy. It's the difficult times that make things interesting.

CHAPTER
Seven

"I am entitled to miracles."

It's Sunday. Blake walks into the kitchen, takes a bite of Alex's toast, and washes it down with Cole's sippy-cup of juice.

"I'm going for a run."

"Now?!"

"Just a quick one," he says with his back to me.

"But I haven't even jumped in the shower!"

"So what's stopping you?"

"But I thought we were going to brunch?"

"Nahhh," he says, shaking his head.

"You can't go now; I need *my* break."

He shrugs his shoulders like *C'mon, get off my back.* Like that will solve it, like that will make the dishes vanish, make the kids stop fighting, make the beds, or take the smell out of my stinky, unwashed hair. And then he is gone and I want to run after him and kill him. No, I want to run in front of him and leave him behind, but it's too late; he has sprinted out the door. Bastard.

I sit down hard on the kitchen chair—defeated. When did we stop looking at each other? Where did all this distance between us come from?

When he comes home, he doesn't like the way I have cleaned up, so he recleans the countertops, the windows, the face of the refrigerator, and the stove. He moves from the kitchen to the dining room. It's not a happy clean; it's a mean, there's-something-bad-on-his-mind clean. I back out slowly and head to the kids' room feeling guilty. I don't get it; what did I do?

The next day, Blake says barely a word to me before he leaves for the office and gives all his kisses and love to the kids, leaving me with nothing. He's in that mood again— cold, stiff, unyielding, and unkind. Any good feelings I have toward him have slipped into the deep hole in my heart. I am about to explode and say, *Hey, I'm over here, the person who makes your meals, takes care of your children, and tends to your needs. You know, the one that gave you time for that great one-hour run yesterday.* But I don't. I watch him slip into his car without saying a word. I try to convince myself it doesn't matter. The good news is, I have another appointment with my therapist. It couldn't have come quickly enough.

My therapist greets me with a smile. Her small frame is hidden under a big white blouse and loose black pants. My therapist doesn't look like my mother, but somehow she reminds me of her. Maybe it's the way she listens to me, or that she gets me, but I think mostly it's the way she makes me feel.

I drop my purse on the floor next to the chair and sit down, and before I can say the things that I have rehearsed in my head on the drive over, she stops me. She makes me close my eyes and take three deep breaths, she makes me slow down, and she makes my spinning mind reduce speed.

But the anger doesn't subside. It's still at the surface when I say, "He cleans and he cleans and cleans and he still doesn't get it right. Then he suffocates me in the imperfection of his own misery. It's strange to see a man clean so much; it seems unnatural, so out of place. And more than just the cleaning, it's *how* he cleans—obsessively. But he thinks he's only doing it to himself; he doesn't get that he's doing it to me too. God, it's so depressing."

She gives me a look that says, *Where did this come from?*

"The tequila brought it out in me."

"Oh?" she asks as she moves her pencil on her yellow pad.

She doesn't get that I'm joking. "No, I'm finally feeling," I say, wrapping my arms around my chest.

"How long did it take?" And she gently wraps her arms around her chest.

"Forever." I can't get comfortable in the chair and try stuffing my hands under my thighs.

"Why haven't you told me this before?"

"I didn't know it was inside of me 'til now. Life is strange that way. It surprises you in the despair of its own abyss."

She nods to let me go on. She hasn't moved an inch in her chair; her eyes are trying to find mine, but I stop looking at her. I'm looking at the desk beyond her. I can't bear to look at her face with what I'm going to say—it's too personal.

"He cleans because he's in pain; his wounds are so deep, so ugly, that he's trying to clean them away. But all that hurt comes to the surface as meanness, as cruelty towards us, towards me, and it's so intense that I want nothing to do with him. I don't want to help him anymore. I don't care what happens to him."

"And?"

"... and it's not the piercing pain that gets to him, that gets to me, it's the weight of it all ... the weight of him. He's too heavy. I can't bear the weight of him anymore."

"What do you mean by cruelty?"

"He's violent." She has no expression when I say this, but I know what she's thinking. "Not physically anymore, but emotionally—not that he's ever hit me, but he has pushed me away, pushed me away hard. He's cruel with his actions—he tears me in two." Now I'm crying. I'm trying so hard not to, but even with all the force that I have to hold them back, the tears run down anyway. I have broken down right in front of her.

She doesn't have to say anything to urge me to continue; I just do. "Marriage is hard because there are times when you're trying to love someone you no longer love. Someone who isn't the person you thought they would be; someone you thought was perfect who's no longer perfect, whose flaws are so in-your-face that you wonder why you married him to begin with. You ask yourself, *Why didn't I see this before* and *Why DID I get married; was it just for the sheer fact of wanting to be married?*" She is looking at me with an expression that invites me to answer my own questions.

But I don't.

"So what holds you together?" she asks.

"One thing and one thing only—the kids."

"You're sure of that?"

"I guess I'm finally seeing things for what they are. Not a fantasy. Not perfect. I'm feeling and it sucks because there are no happy feelings right now. I'm feeling the loss of what I thought I had."

My mind slips to yesterday. I tell her, "We can't live our life in such a clean house. It's unnatural. To have a cleaning person come so many times in a month, and have such a sterile environment—it's not normal. Floors so clean that you could eat off of them … and I'm talking about the one in the *garage*. It's abnormal to have your kids watch television instead of play, and I mean *really* play—like make a fort in the center of the living room—because the mess will bother him." I'm not looking at her when I say, "There's a rage that hides so deep inside of him that if he let it go it might kill you, it's *that* ugly, *that* intense." Now I meet her gaze.

"The kids built this fort made out of every spare blanket and pillow in the house, and it was *so* cool that suddenly all their stuffed animals and all their books were inside to share the coziness. Yeah, to an untrained eye it looked like a heap, to Blake it looked like a heap, a mess that grated on his nerves because he couldn't clean it up fast enough, he can't be rid of it in a nanosecond. They made a place where dreaming comes from. I don't think Blake is capable of dreaming, only cleaning." She knows I'm rambling, so she brings me back to center.

"And what was it that you thought you had with Blake?"

"Love," I say straight to her eyes.

"And do you have it?" Her face goes soft.

"No and yes. I'm gaining it for myself but losing it from him. Is that possible?"

"It's the same thing."

"What do you mean?"

"When you gain your own power, you drain the power

from the original source, from where you thought you were getting it."

"Well that sucks," I say, but without really processing what she has said. "Are you saying ... I was getting power from him?"

"Yes, you were getting power from him."

"But now I realize I have my own so I've cut him off? I was letting him take my power because I gave it to him?"

"Yes."

"Why has it taken so long to get it?"

"Relax, it's not a race."

"Okay. I got it. So it's okay to hate him?"

"Absolutely."

"So it's okay not to buy into his guilt?"

"Exactly. Just be yourself. Just be and it will be okay."

"Why can't I forgive him? Why does it take so long to forgive him?"

"It takes as long as it takes."

Eight

"Let miracles replace all grievances."

Katie found her way back to herself first. She said it happened because she was open to it. It was more than that; it was all her constant work on herself— the meditation, yoga, journaling, good hygiene, and disciplined self-discovery. More specifically, I think it was *A Course in Miracles*—she opened it daily. It saved her life more than once, and later magically found its way into my life and saved me too.

A Course in Miracles is a self-study course that teaches the relinquishment of fear and the acceptance of love. A guide to provide a way to one's own Internal Teacher—the God or Eternal Love within. Not everyone believes that God lives within us. Katie and I grew up thinking and believing that God is separate from us—that He lives in Heaven and not in our hearts. But once I experienced not being separate from God, my life was different, Katie's even more so.

Katie's spirituality grew from her very own space, her personal space—her "place of solace and divine intervention." A place where her kids couldn't put their toys, clothes, school stuff, and crumbs. A space where her husband couldn't leave his dirty underwear, papers, briefcase, or squash racket. It was a special place away from noise, chatter, clutter, and voices. A place so quiet it was easy to slip into meditation. She found refuge in her sanctuary ... She found it in the garage. It was perfect—the only place where she could hide and not be interrupted, where she could go to be cut off from the main artery of the family, the constant in-your-face heartbeat. The garage was crammed to the gills with bikes, skateboards, boots, gardening tools, Jack's workbench, and of course the cars. But her sacred spot wasn't next to the water heater, or in between the extra refrigerator and the garden hose. It wasn't next to the only tiny window above the garbage cans either. It was up the pull-out stairs in the crawlspace where all the Christmas stuff and other odds and ends were stored.

It was an odd-shaped room that luckily you could stand up in—the size of a large walk-in closet, hot and stuffy, and badly in need of a window. But it was large enough for an easel, a stool, an overstuffed chair, a small table that housed her altar, and room to stretch and do yoga.

It didn't happen overnight, but great things never do. It took longer than she hoped to clear out the mess and find new places for the stuff that didn't get thrown away. It also took time to find the right paint color to make the makeshift studio warm and bright. It took even longer to fix the amenities, like wiring for lights and music, and to find all the right accessories.

Jack objected. Trying to convince him to get the window installed was a waste of time. He wasn't cheap, and, yes, they could afford the window. It was the idea that threatened him. Why could she have her dream space when he hadn't found his? He eventually came around—he had no choice. She had found the strength and courage to do what was best for her on her own. But more importantly, she had found her gift; it was stifled so deeply in her soul that when it came up it gasped and grabbed like it was her last breath.

When the room was finally done, it was heaven. The newly installed window was key. It was huge, and the morning light flickered in through the trees, making her new space feel like a tree house. She nestled into the nooks and crannies of her new space like a second skin and began to paint. Paint and paint. Oils and acrylics, sometimes pastels. The art classes she had been taking over the years had opened up her gift, and what now poured out was unbridled talent. She was better than good; she was great, and it's not just because I love her. The galleries in Dana Point and Manhattan Beach proved it. They said she could be a one-name artist.

She thought she had nothing to give outside her family. Oh, but she did. She gave beauty, and finally, yes *finally*, she began to understand how amazing she was.

It was a Friday, the day that closes out the stress of the week and opens to the fun of the weekend. Traffic is murder on Friday, so when Katie invited Cole and me up to witness her new space, we agreed that staying for dinner and traveling down to San Diego when the flow of traffic became bearable made the most sense.

Cole and I climbed up the steps to her studio. I placed him on the floor and flopped into the overstuffed chair. "This place is really great. Who would have thought it?"

"It's my wholly place, where I get whole and find my heart."

"Can you believe how much the window opened it up?" Cole is eager to look around, touching everything with his chubby, sausage fingers and leaving prints on the window pane. The sun picks up the highlights in his hair, and his tender movements mesmerize me. *What a gentle soul—how did I get so lucky?*

"It's better than I thought it would be," she says looking around slowly. A satisfied smile creeps across her face.

Underneath the window is her yoga mat, the perfect spot to soak up the sun while she practiced the ancient system of stretching and balancing. She tells me that yoga has brought her to this place of self-control and well-being. She says it's more than building body strength and flexibility; it's what gives her enhanced mental clarity. I believe her, though I've never tried it; I'd rather go burn and churn at a kickboxing class.

CHAPTER
Nine

"Miracles are seen in light, and light and strength are one."

I grab Cole, kiss his sun-drenched head, climb down from Katie's studio, and head straight to the kitchen. There's no need to rush home.

Blake had agreed to take Alex to soccer practice right after picking him up from school. Thanks to my work with the therapist, I had asked him to step up to more parenting duties, and he complied—a lucky first.

To Blake, there was nothing wrong in his marriage other than not enough sex. He couldn't see that his own evolution was being tested and that the lack of it was catching up with him. He thought he was just being asked to spend more time with his kids; challenges loomed. Bumpy roads have a way of kicking up stones into your eye.

When my therapist advised me to get Blake to do more with the kids, Blake complied because he wasn't going to therapy and didn't want to be the bad guy. This made for more time for me, which made hanging out with Katie more enjoyable. My therapist's tactic was that if I was having fun in my life and feeling more empowered, I would be more desirable at home. Or so we thought.

As I washed my hands at the kitchen sink, Katie stood three inches from my face. "Oh my God, what is *that* on your chin?"

"Oh, that … It's my fly hair," I say, turning away from her to wipe my hands.

"Your what?"

"You know, like the movie with Jeff Goldblum when he turns into the fly and all those coarse hairs grow out of his body. I've got one."

"Yeah, I'd say so. Have you thought about plucking it?" I give her an exasperated look. *Oh, you think I should? I never thought of that.* "Of course I pluck it! I guess I waited too long." *Why is she doing this to me?*

"Here, let me get the tweezers," she says, handing me the wooden spoon so I can stir the pesto.

"You mean you don't even have one fly hair?" I say incredulously. "I thought everyone had at least *one* fly hair somewhere. Maybe yours is on your B-U-T-T and it's just that you've never seen it."

"Fat chance."

Knowing Katie she was probably right. Blondes—they get nothing bad.

Cole has wrapped his arms around my leg. He hugs tight without a word and then walks away—melting my heart again.

She comes at me with the tweezers and asks, "So what do you think about the affirmation walk?" We are back on our topic of spirituality and movement—a conversation that has been interrupted by Cole knocking over the set of water glasses at the table. But before we can continue, in ambles Jack. Taking a peak inside the refrigerator, he utters a quiet, "Hello, ladies."

Jack's sculptured features used to be strong and confident but now have gone soft. His thick hair is parted to the side and was once light brown but is rapidly going grey—marriage does that. Jack's best feature is still his green eyes. They can take your breath away; that is, if you can see them through the thick glasses he rarely takes off. I've always seen what Katie sees in him but have never been attracted to him—it would feel like incest.

He flicks off his custom-made leather shoes that cost just under a grand and I'm thinking, *Are you kidding? Do you know how many pairs of shoes I could buy for the same money?*

Katie and I try to pick up our conversation on spirituality. I offer, "I like the idea of a God that doesn't live in my thoughts but could be seen with the naked eye."

Jack interrupts, "What came first: the need of God or God?"

Silence.

He continues, "Why do some people hear and know God, while others don't believe He's there at all?"

Silence. *We didn't invite you into our conversation*, I think to myself. Now I feel self-conscious. He is there interjecting. I liked it better when he was just an accessory to the kitchen table.

He has now taken off his coat and set it carefully on a chair next to the table. "When you wake up, do you wonder why you're here in the first place? Maybe those who don't believe in God have a chemical imbalance; maybe it's genetic. There are scientists who believe that human spirituality is an adaptive trait. I think spiritual beliefs are hardwired to genes, in my case missing. *Nemo dat quod non ha*bet." No one gives what he doesn't have.

I don't know why he said what he just said, but I wish he'd leave. If you didn't know him you'd think that he was mad—mad at the world, mad at something. Instead, he's just tired from a long day at work.

Katie adds penne to the boiling water. Her daughter, Samantha, has poked her head in the kitchen, wondering when dinner will be ready. She is an eye-rolling, gum-snapping teen, still dressed in her school uniform, and as soon as she is there, she is gone. Her younger brother, Jack Jr., is quietly playing with his Erector Set upstairs. Katie stirs the pasta and retorts, "I think it's something that you have to work on."

"How?" he snorts.

I just realize he never gave her a kiss hello, nor his *Mellita, domi adsum*—Honey, I'm home.

Katie moves to her point: "Meditation or prayer." Samantha is back in the kitchen, and as she looks at her father, I realize they have not acknowledged one another. He is like an ornament in the room, not the father whom she loves.

"What will that do?" he says, adjusting his pants to cross his legs so his balls don't get crushed by the Italian wool blend. Now he has baited her—testing the waters, testing her expertise on the subject. She is ready for combat. "There are studies showing brain activity while meditating or praying. More specifically, the deeper someone descends into a meditative state, the more active the frontal lobe and limbic system become, like a flash of life. The source of rapture and deep feelings comes alive. And at the same time the parietal lobe at the back of the brain, the place where we orient time and space, shuts down. The boundaries of

self fall away and the feeling of oneness arises. If you want
a religious or spiritual experience, try meditating. I don't
think you need a spiritual gene." She has moved on to washing the lettuce and stops to take out the garlic bread, which
is browned to perfection.

He has finally loosened his tie—Prada—which looked
like it was strangling him. Maybe *he* will loosen up now too.
And when did he go designer? He bends down to pick up his
shoes and says, "Maybe the God experience is man's paci-
fier, so that he doesn't have to fear the inevitable—death."
Now he places his black briefcase on the bench beside me,
not thinking that he is invading my space. No, it is I who
am invading his; this is his house, after all. I get on the floor
with Cole and start picking up his toys. I never thought
Jack was the expensive name-brand type. Maybe it's a work
thing. Maybe he's making more money. I feel like I don't
know him anymore.

Katie retorts, "Grace is available to everyone. A spiritual
journey has never been about the big bang or a burning
bush. It's about the slow and steady experience where there
are occasional beams of light."

"I guess I'm looking for something real. What's for dinner?" he asks as he walks to the stove and takes a whiff
while giving her a disapproving eye.

This is the same guy who once arrived at Katie's apartment with a large gift in hand. It was wrapped so that each
seam was crisp and tight—you could tell he wanted it to
be absolutely flawless when she received it. Inside was an
expensive astronomy book, oversized and heavy, a sleeping
bag for two, and a flashlight with a card that read, "How
about a date under the stars?"

I study his face before he turns to go upstairs to change.
The kitchen light above casts a shadow on his cheek, which

looks like a smudge. The shadow was thin, yet polite. It didn't expose things that you didn't want to see right away. It covered the things that make people vain and mean. He wasn't a bad person, he was just lost. He had forgotten about the light inside.

CHAPTER

Ten

"Let me be still and listen to the truth."

K atie picked an upscale coffee shop to meet at, and I waited for her. After my first sip of tea I began to unwind and relax; Cole was with a babysitter, and Alex was at school.

The lighting was muted and emanated from lamps of all sizes and shapes. They were scattered around the room on mismatched end tables that looked like they came from a high-end flea market. There was an oversize, worn, Oriental rug in the center of the floor and over-stuffed furniture in sage velour—something you might see in an upscale living room—that probably came from the same flea market.

At the table closest to me sat a man intently reading a newspaper. He looked like a normal guy: medium height and weight, glasses, dressed in casual clothing. If it weren't for his table companions, he might be a college student, a computer programmer … just a plain Joe. But the fact that he shared the table with two small boys and a woman made the scene so strange. The table was cut into two sections by his newspaper, which he hid behind until he spoke, his tone disconnected as if he were trying to be something he wasn't. His presence seemed like a favor he was granting them, a way of appeasing them when all he really wanted to do was be by himself, doing his thing, doing his thing alone.

"How is it?" he asks the smaller boy, maybe 2 ½ years old, who is about to take a bite out of his chocolate-covered banana.

The boy is oblivious to his father and his question; he is in chocolate bliss and doesn't care if his father connects with him or not. He is already connected with God and the Universe and his banana and is so simply pure and in the sacred moment of delight, or at least is having one heck of a chocolate high ...

The wife of course is doing everything. Taking the wrapper off treats, getting the napkins, opening the milk carton, making sure the smaller child won't fall out of the seat. She's doing five things at once and the man's doing one thing: reading the newspaper, which creates a wall between them, dividing the space into his own personal office and the miniature daycare that apparently has none of his concern. It is presented as a single accident, something outside of and separate from me, but it is something more deliberate—a reminder that there are no accidents, and I am not alone in the effects of my life.

Who is this man who wears glasses so thick that they make him look smart? He is a typical father who thinks of taking care of his needs first, having his own moment, while the mother attends and gives selflessly her space, her time, her love, and her connection to life to make sure her children are well cared for.

Or is she the enigma trapped in a role of service and unconditional giving, giving too much, and giving it all away. The father is better off in more ways than one: his children are happy, he is happy. His wife is exhausted, and it's her own fault ... And things begin to come into focus for me.

In my mind I thank my therapist, my best friend, and God for bringing me back to me, for helping me see things outside of myself, things outside of my bubble.

I am less consumed by my own world as I take another sip of tea, breathe in through my nose, and hear the air come into my body. I see people around me: I can look around and really *see* other people, not just a foot sticking out from a table or the back of someone's head as they read the paper.

Then Katie walks in. "Sorry I'm late."

"You're not late, you're right on time."

She puts down her purse and takes off a pale green cotton sweater. She sits down to let out a breath. "Thanks," she says when she sees the herbal tea bag in a mug, hot water in a small pot beside the cup. She pours the water over the tea bag, and her shoulders relax.

As she is pouring, I feel compelled to tell her about my life. "I still feel wedged. Trapped between wanting the things from the past and fantasizing about the future. Where did my self-confidence go? I used to be on top of the world!" I lament.

"You still are."

"But can I still bitch anyway?"

"Oh, God yes."

"Blake and I speak different languages. We don't know how to recognize one another. I think there was a time where we loved everything about each other. Now his faults glare in my face too brightly to see—like I'm caught in high

beams. How do you unite your heart with someone you feel
so disconnected from?" I ask her, but I don't want an answer yet. "There was a time when he wanted to hear everything I had to say. Now he cuts me off, so I have to repeat
myself and he hears it as nagging." Katie puts down her
cup and is looking at me. The expression on her face tells
me she's about to give advice, but I don't let her. I look past
her to the table with the family as they prepare to go, then I
add what I think she is going to say: "So I am separate, so I
need to work on myself more, is that it?" But I don't let her
answer. "Strange; the better I feel about myself, the less I
want to take care of him." Katie lets me go on and on and I
know I'm sounding like a broken record but she still hears
me and waits until I finally stop.

"You know men aren't mind readers even though we
want them to be," she reminds me. "The space between the
hemispheres in their brains is wider than ours—it's tougher
for them to feel everything that we do." She takes a sip of
her tea. I feel the warmth of my cup on my cold fingertips,
and I take in the buzz of new people who have just en-
tered the shop. "You have to spell it out for men if there
is a specific result you're looking for. You can't give them
hints—not subtle, not even strong and obvious—you just
have to say it. And it sucks because we wish they had more
mystery and intuition, but they don't."

She's right, but I don't want her to be.

"You can create your own life, moment to moment, day
to day," she goes on. "Just because he does things that an-
noy you doesn't mean you have to get overwhelmed by his
actions or manners. Go deeper. Live from a space so deep
inside that it cannot be violated, tainted, or touched. That
place in your heart that is sacred, full of unconditional love
and acceptance."

"You actually think that's easy?"

"Yes."

"No way."

"Yep. Once you go there, you can go back ... and back and back. Then it becomes a way of life. If you once loved him unconditionally, you can do it again."

"Uh-huh." *Yeah, right.*

"Stop looking to receive something. Giving is a gift in itself and it will heal you. I know when I give a hundred percent of myself I feel exhilarated, but when I give only a part of myself, I feel drained."

"I specialize in drained."

"Give purely. So the giving is an extension of you—the God in you. We radiate more than a million suns, so don't give with just one ray of light, give with all the rays that you are. You will be received so warmly and get so much more back."

I try to take it in. I try to visualize what she says, but it seems too far away, too far-fetched. "You know that all *sounds* good, but how do you do it? How do you give like that when you feel like you have nothing left?"

"Fill yourself up. Fill yourself up, so you are overflowing the maximum of your soul. Give to yourself first; treat yourself with the love that you are made of. Honor, worship, and enjoy yourself to the fullest. Look at the sun, really look at the sun, let your eyes burn a little and then multiply that light by a million. That is what you are made of—white, golden light, a piece of God."

"That sounds so conceited."

"It's the opposite."

"Okay. So how are you?"

"Great," she says too joyously. She looks like she's telling the truth, but somehow I don't believe her.

But on the way home I do look at the sun briefly and the light is too bright and I think of that light even stronger—a millionfold. I place that light in the center of my heart. And then something shifts. I feel happy for a single moment.

CHAPTER
Eleven

"Truth will correct all errors in my mind."

I have to tell myself that the work I'm doing is good work even though it is hard and hardly noticed. No one seems to be getting that—even my therapist.

Blake sits in the chair in front of me in his business attire; it is his lunch break and he's come straight from work. His legs are crossed at his ankles. My therapist sits to my right. Light comes through the sheer curtains; my mind is muddled, but I can see daylight through the clods of dirt that fill my life.

We are now a couple at my therapist's office—*our* therapist's office. We're in marriage counseling, and I am mad at both of them. She is coaching Blake, and I can't believe what she has just said: "Well, Blake, you do have the job." I hear her saying, *You have the* real *job*.

Blake replies, "And you can't do it all, like they want you to." He then realizes I'm in the room, and I give him an

I'm-going-to-kill-you-in-your-sleep look. He pretends that he was joking, and now he's thinking, *Where did her sense of humor go?* I would reply, if it were a real conversation, *Down the drain with our sex life.*

My therapist of all people has turned on me and is on *his* side. I look at her desk and there are pictures of her kids. She is a mother, for God's sake. *What the hell is wrong with her?* But she's on the enemy's side. Female traitor! She doesn't get it because she is a therapist—someone with a real job and a real salary, a two-hundred-dollar-an-hour paycheck. And what do I get an hour? Monopoly money. She can buy her own clothes without asking her husband for money. Her job gains recognition and uses her intellect and is regarded as something noble. She's not getting the nobility in my job.

I pick up clues that the therapist thinks I'm useless when she says, "So, Blake, go ahead. You had to stay late at work because you had no other option ..." She looks at me and nods her head as if to say, *You can learn from this,* and *Pick up a new skill, learn a new language, take a class,* while my mind responds, *What's wrong with the way I live my life, and when did you get so mean?*

Blake crosses his legs at the knee—unlike some men, he looks masculine when he does this—and then the Wicked Witch of the West does likewise, mirroring his body language to make him feel even more comfortable, and I want to roll my eyes *so* badly, but I don't. She has stopped reminding me of my mother.

She interrupts her verbal lovemaking with Blake, looks straight into my eyes, and begins to lecture me. "Our self-protecting impulses can block the love we crave—but we don't have to let them." I want to say, *Shut up with the "You're not doing what you're supposed to" crap, you heartless, un-loving, mother hussy. Give me a break, I'm stuck here.* But she wouldn't get it; she would just think that I wasn't listening. Which I wasn't—at least I wasn't *liking* what I was listening to.

Her arms lie in her lap in the same fashion as Blake's as she adds, "Have you noticed that you have attached your happiness to external forces? Does your state of mind rely solely on someone else? The only person you are in control of is you."

I want to tell her about his selfishness—like the day I was pregnant with Cole, and Alex was three and home sick with the flu. The kind of sick that made him irritable and needy, the kind of sick that talks back, and screams, and is mean. I was not only pregnant, I also had food poisoning and was retching my guts out. I called Blake and begged him to come home early to help me out. Katie was away with her family—I had no one else to turn to, so why not turn to my husband, right?

He flat-out said, "No. I have work to do. I can't just get up and leave because you're not feeling well." I hated him so much that day. I would have come home for him. But I can't tell my therapist this story and all the others that make him the bad guy because she thinks *I* am the problem. Bitch.

I'm sick of listening to her, and I look out the window behind her and start to zone out. I check myself out of the room without their even knowing it. I push away the thoughts of how my husband and therapist have joined forces and try to relax my breathing; I go right into the leaves of the tree outside the window and begin to daydream.

Staying home with my kids isn't a bad thing. It's a privilege, especially when they are prophets for life. I look at them in my mind's eye and let the lovebirds talk as I drift away to what does work at our home—the kids. I think back to a couple of days before, when both boys were running their Matchbox cars over a chair, making *vroom, vroom* and tire screeching sounds. I could see them in the hallway mirror that allowed me to watch them without being noticed.

Alex says to his younger brother, "Do it this way." And it sounds too bossy, like me. As I think to myself, *I wish he wouldn't talk that way,* I wish I wouldn't either.

Cole steals the car from Alex's hand.

Alex retorts, "Hey, that's mine."

"Now mine," Cole says, taking the car down to the carpet and using its pattern as a road.

"Mom!"

I don't say anything; my parenting books say to make them work these things out on their own.

"MOM!" Alex screams but soon realizes I am not coming. So he grabs the car back and Cole bites him. This is the moment when he wants to bite Cole back, wants to manhandle him, and I want to step in. But I don't, and Alex does something spectacular.

He understands, understands that Cole is not strong with using his words, understands that if he does bite him back, I will come in and it won't be fun and he still wants to play. So he lets out a breath and says, "Fine. Do it your way." He picks up another car and goes on playing, happy like nothing has happened, like the teeth marks on his wrist don't hurt.

I wish I could do that—be that loving and tolerant or just let my hurt go.

But I am not. And all the wrong things that I do as a mom show up when I don't want them to, when I want to get a moment right, and all my flaws come screaming through. Like when my kids want to make something that is messy and things get out of control. I want to be a fun mom, a cool mom, but something gets lost in the translation. The boys drag chairs across the hardwood kitchen floors so they can reach the countertops easily. I've put Saran Wrap over the counters for easy cleanup. And when the measuring spoons come out, we are still having fun. But when the first ingredients are poured, I have to gently urge them off their chairs because the milk, even though it is "so wet and cold and fun" to feel, is not so cool when it gets places it's not supposed to be, like on the parts of the counter that aren't covered, like on the floor and my clothes. If I'm not careful, the recipe won't be perfect.

And when prodding Cole and Alex down off their chairs doesn't work, I have to be more forceful so things will stay clean. "Okay boys, that's enough, no, stop, stop, stop, too much sugar … no, no … no, no no, not like that, no slow down, too much, stop, stop … here let me do it. You can watch for the next time." Knowing full well there would be no next time. This is a messy job, not for kids.

Back in my therapist's office, I look at Blake and I can tell by his relaxed face that he feels understood; finally someone gets him. I want to puke. I am sick of his incessant whining; he makes the same face Cole makes.

Yesterday morning when I was in the shower for the first time in days, every toy imaginable was out on the bathroom floor to entice Cole to play, giving me a second to feel the water wash my body clean. But that would be too easy, too well thought out for him to actually stay and play under my watchful, relaxed eye. Leave toys out so he can stay put and I can get clean. That never happens. Why would he go for the toys when there are better things to do? He heads right for the drawer with all the things that should be marked DANGER! STAY AWAY IF YOU CANNOT READ THIS SIGN.

He detaches the baby lock and goes right for the nose hair trimmers, which he proceeds to put in his mouth. One step out of the shower, dripping puddles at my feet, I see him reach for the toenail clippers; as I get close to him, he decides to taste those too. He screams because he wants them so badly. I try to ignore his screeching and tears and think of his safety.

After I wipe off the bathroom floor so Cole doesn't slip, I return to the warm shower and he finds my toothbrush and toothpaste. He is trying to do it by himself—he is trying to be independent and act big. The toothbrush is on the floor, and both hands are squeezing out the toothpaste with super-human strength as I coach from inside the shower, "Gentle. Okay, honey, that's good, that's enough."

"Mommy I do," he says with a curled brow, just like his father's in therapy. He finally stops with a dog-turd-size glob on the floor and a spattering of mint gel on the brush.

He is happy—just another day in pigpen toddler heaven. I decide to clean it when I get out. He brushes his teeth, I begin to relax, and then the cat walks in. He is now brushing the cat with my toothbrush, and then he drops the tooth-brush and runs after her.

It's not the cat I am worried about, the cat who will have her tail, ears and large clumps of flesh pulled. Nor am I worried that my sweet child may be scratched, because our cat has never defended herself in this way. It's not the tooth-paste turd that I have to clean when I am finally clean. After all, he's so cute—really cute. What I'm worried about is what will happen when I can't see him. So I quickly dry my-self off, clean the bathroom floor and throw the toothbrush in the drawer. It's the next day that's not so cute, when I go to brush my teeth and end up spitting out cat hair.

The therapist gives me a smile of *Well done. Good job*

letting your husband speak. "Thanks for being such an active listener," she says to me before letting us go. She doesn't realize I haven't heard a word he has said, but I take the compliment anyway.

Twelve

"Peace to my mind. Let all my thoughts be still."

Back home it's another perfect March day—or so I think: sunshine, no clouds, no humidity and seventy-three degrees with a light breeze. The leaves on the eucalyptus trees beside our house rustle slightly, leaving a healing fragrance in the air, richer than a Halls cough drop.

I try to create some type of joy in my head, but I am not even healed by the smell of eucalyptus; I'm stuck again! Not stuck in the heart, stuck in the head. The perfect weather doesn't make me feel calm or relaxed; my head spins round and round while my heart is so jammed—so naturally I obsess about it: about why I can't fix my heart, why I can't be happy on such a fine day. So now my head is stuck and I'm miserable, heavy, feeling sucked into a dark hole of guilt and remorse. Even easygoing Cole irritates me; I can't wait until he goes down for a nap.

But the truth is, I'm stuck because I suck. When morning

started I felt perfect, whole, and complete, and it changed when I tried to do something special. I was going to make blueberry pancakes for breakfast. Both boys were fighting colds and sleep deprived, which increased the whining and neediness quotient beyond the edge of human kindness.

Alex screeched, arms flailing, "That's my toy!" and yanked it out of his brother's hand. Cole tumbled back and fell hard on his bum and started to cry. But he's an older, wiser toddler and goes back to his stolen toy with a high-frequency scream. The boys cannot get out of each other's space and they hate being near each other. The griddle is too hot; the pancakes are charcoal brown on the outside and gummy raw the inside—inedible. The shrieks and crying reached such outrageous levels that dead monks in the Himalayas could have heard them.

The kids were hungry and I was at my wits' end, and when they wouldn't stop squealing or listen to any of my instructions, I screamed at the top of my lungs, sending fear into their tiny beings and inspiring huge tears of liquid fright—like I had changed the fiber of who they were, like I was Satan.

Then I was sick with what I did, and I cried. And when Alex said, "It's okay, Mommy. It's okay, we're sorry," I cried even harder and stronger. He then hugged my thighs and begged, "Please stop crying." They were only being kids who were hungry, sick, and tired. They didn't have to be sorry; I was the one who should be apologizing.

I call Katie from the black retro phone that looks like the one Mrs. Cleaver used to call her best friend Jan. But this wasn't a conversation about baking cookies.

"I suck, I really suck." I start to choke up.

"Why?" she asked softly.

"I don't think I'm a good mom."

"What are you talking about?"

"I lost it."

"And—"

"And I screamed at my kids this morning, and it scared them and I saw what I did and I can't stand myself because of it."

"Okay. Slow down and tell me what happened."

So I did. "And then do you know what Alex said? Do you want to know what he asked me?"

"What?" her voice is kind and gentle.

"He asked, 'Mommy, why are you so angry?' And I looked at him and, oh, God, he was so right, and I felt horrible. I'm this horrible angry monster. I can't do this anymore, I can't be a mom. I'm no good at it."

"Oh shut up!" she says in a way to make me laugh, but it has zero effect.

"I'm serious!"

"So you think anger is a bad thing?"

"Yes."

"That's where you are wrong; anger is as normal and natural as joy. It's a part of us. It's just all about how you use it."

"Well, I obviously don't know how. Now my kids are going to be in therapy for the rest of their lives. Should I go punch a pillow first?"

"No, no, no. All that's just a rehearsal for how to blow your anger out of proportion. It starts with a breath and ends with a breath. It's like this ..."

I interrupt her. "How do I connect my heart to my children and let them know that I love them without feeling *everything* they feel, only more so. How do you minimize the connection so that you don't go crazy?"

"You don't give yourself away. You give them the compassion and love that come from your heart, but you don't give them your whole heart. You can put a magic shield up so that your heart doesn't slip out. You keep your heart open, and open it larger and larger to the universe, and the universe will give it back multiplied. When you love fully from your heart, good comes back—cause and effect."

"You keep on saying that crap. I need specifics. How do you do that exactly?" I have now stopped twisting the curlicue cord of the phone and moved on to my hair. I find a good piece at the back, above my neck, and twist over and over. The piece is as thin as a pencil and it's smooth, silky. I twirl to make a knot but the knot slips out like it's supposed to. My hair makes me feel calmer, or at least it tries.

"Here are a couple of ideas: You try to work it out before it gets out of hand. You put your hands on their shoulders and you get at eye level and you make them work it out. Kids respond so well to touch. You say something like, 'Alex, you seem really frustrated right now. How are you going to ask Cole for what you want?' And then you help Cole with his words and offer him what to say, like, 'Stop. I don't like that.'"

"Okay, so where do you get the wings when that doesn't work?"

"You breathe deeper and deeper 'til your mind becomes still and you find a little peace, so they stop sucking your heart out. If they continue wanting and over-needing you, you leave the room, you lock yourself in the bathroom and put in ear plugs, or you run water and wash your face, you look at yourself in the mirror and you breathe in light, love, energy that comes from God, and you ask for help and you expect some grace."

"It's like I can't shut my brain off. I start spinning and my anger blurts out. How do I shut my brain off?"

"I know, I know. It's about practice and catching it sooner, before you want to explode."

"But how do you shut your brain off?" I am still twisting and twisting my hair; this time I found a better piece next to my ear, well-conditioned and soft.

She begins to tell me a story about a prophet. She explains that the story has the answers to all the hard questions in life:

This prophet goes to God and says, "God, I found this evil, this fear-based black evil that I have to get rid of so man doesn't hurt himself." And God says, "Yes, that is a problem." And the prophet says, "I know—I'll go hide it so man can't find it." He takes it to the highest mountain and says, "Here, God, what do you think?" And God answers, "Man is very curious and strong. He will climb the mountain and find it." So the prophet takes the fear-based evil to the bottom of the deepest sea and says, "What about now, My Lord?" And God says, "Man is very motivated and will build a submarine and find it." So the prophet takes it to the middle of the largest desert and starts digging a hole and says, "How about here?" And God says, "Man can be very persistent and will find it there." So the prophet says, "I know, I'll put it in man's mind; he'll never find it there." And God says, "Perfect."

"Okay, so how do you take it out?"

"You don't shut your brain off—and you don't shut your emotions off either. How you tame your angry and overwhelming feelings of evil frustration when they are at a 7 out of 10 or higher is you don't breathe—you'll be adding fuel to the fire. Don't breathe, don't hit a pillow. AMD instead."

"What? Wait, you always say I should breathe. I thought that's what's supposed to calm me down!"

"Not when you're that angry and spinning. If you concentrate on breathing, you'll fuel the fire."

She's right. Breathing doesn't work when I'm that worked up.

"AMD. Action, movement, and distraction. Let's say you're in the kitchen and you're cleaning up the kids' mess and they throw food at you and you don't laugh but they keep on horsing around and won't listen. If you can't laugh at them or breathe through it to get yourself calm, right then you tell them, 'I need a moment. I'll be right back,' and you go away from them and actually do something. You water the plants, take the garbage out, cut flowers, do a physical task and do it 'til you've completely calmed down."

Touchdown. I got it. She had finally reached me. *Okay, I need to start breathing, and when I've lost my chance to collect myself, I AMD.* "Why can't I stop obsessing about not being a good enough mom?"

"Because you are a good mom."

"No, I'm serious."

"About the mom stuff or the obsessing stuff?"

"Katie!"

"Tate, you have a hot cingulate gyrus."

"What?!"

"The brain's gear shifter; it gets stuck, we all get stuck!"

"Really?"

"Really."

"You know, there's nothing wrong with teaching your kids to give *themselves* a kiss and a hug, to wrap their *own* arms around themselves and squeeze. You can't always get there to kiss every boo-boo. Especially when you need to be taken care of first. If you take care of yourself first, they will learn to take care of *themselves* first as well."

The sun is bright and reflects off the kitchen window, too bright but not blinding. Katie has done it again—shifted my perception of my life. On the kitchen table is a pedestal bowl filled with fresh fruit, green grapes flowing over the edge like water. We say goodbye, I put the handset in the cradle of the phone, and I sink into the chair to take it all in. Cole climbs into my lap and rests his head on my chest.

CHAPTER
Thirteen

"Fear is not justified in any form."

The following day, after countless months of therapeutic phone calls and sessions in Katie's kitchen, she calls to ask if she can come down to San Diego. She arrives just as I finish changing a poopy diaper, wipe my hands clean, pull up Cole's navy pants and let him run free. He heads for his inside scooter. It is a ruby red Radio Flyer with thick rubber wheels that don't leave marks on the hardwood floor.

The sun shines weakly through the trees into the family room. He scoots and makes puttering sounds as I sink into the chocolate-brown leather sofa and watch him. Katie hasn't said a word since she arrived.

"So update me on your latest paintings," I say as she sits across from me on the couch.

With a straight and serious face, looking right into my eyes, she says, "Jack has cancer."

"What?!"

"Yeah." She doesn't look at me now, and I am too stunned to move. She has turned her head and is looking out the sliding-glass door.

"Oh my God," I barely whisper. I put my hand on her forearm, but she moves from under my touch. "When did you find out?"

"It just happened," she says, dropping her eyes to the floor and shaking her head. "It's lymphoma."

"How is he?"

"Needy. Can we talk about something else?" Stunned. "Sure." If Cole wasn't in the room making puttering and crashing sounds there would be complete silence. He is there and not there at the same time as my mind spins.

"I need quick, hot, naughty sex. No rules," she says, tossing her hair.

"Okay?"

"Not with my husband!"

"You're kidding, right?"

"Do you have to take everything so literally? I'm having a little daydream here. Should I sprinkle Viagra over his meal?"

I feel paralyzed. "Whose meal?" She's looking at her French manicure when I ask, "The guy in your fantasy?"

"Nah, all you have to do is dress to thrill—Victoria's."

If she still smoked she would be lighting up a cigarette right then, taking a first drag and then giving off that same faraway look that comes with a first exhale.

"Why is it the best fantasies are those we've never indulged in? I want that man who doesn't ask if he can have sex but takes me without asking, carries me up to my bedroom, rips my clothes away with his teeth and places my hand over his heart so that I can feel the beating ... pounding. I mean, who explores not just with his fingertips but with the back of his hands, rubbing my hip bones slowly with his knuckles to remind me that there are still places on my body where you can find a bone under all this fat. Maybe I should just whip my vibrator out." This is from the woman who I actually thought loved her husband all the time. Her sex life was so active you'd think she was a tantric aerobics teacher. And if there were such a thing, she would be the one with her class filled to the rim with men of all ages—she would *be* the Viagra.

"This is too weird. Can we talk about Jack?"

"He's got cancer, all right!"

My voice is soft. "But, how are *you?* How is *he?* Can we talk about this a little?"

She ignores me. "Yes the vibrator, to some the only sex available. I stopped using it after Sam found it and started to play with it at six. Then Jack Jr. asked what it was, and then *he* was playing with it, rubbing it all over his face and on Sam's tummy. So you can see why I had to get rid of it ... Do you think we still have that glow in the morning, or do we look old like they do?"

"What do you mean? You think Jack is looking old?" I'm thinking it's probably from the cancer.

"Doesn't Blake?"

"No ... I don't know."

"I hope I still have the glow. I hope I don't look old and prune-faced. I think the reason our marriage has worked is that we went in with such low expectations and knew it would be hard work. Maybe we had insight before we got married, living in sin for all those years. I dunno. I guess I just wish that in a million years from now I can be close, an arm's length away, and still have amazing things to say about Jack."

I'm now chewing on the end of my hair, a good piece from the nape. I think she has gone psycho—she's not making any sense. Maybe the scars from her childhood are the source of all this crazy talk.

She has bent over to the coffee table and taken a tiny bite out of one of Cole's Cheerios. "I wish he would shed the tie and shed some pounds. There was a time when he was obsessed about a perfect stomach; now he's getting saggy, back there too. What do I say to the guy, 'Hey, you're turning into a lard ass!' It's not like my boobs are where they were when we got married. I shouldn't be complaining; I still can't fit into the pair of jeans I wore when we were dating and somehow he can, or at least he makes me think he can."

Cole gets off the scooter and runs toward me. He starts grabbing at my face; he senses how tense I am. He then cuddles into my lap as I give him a hug, then I put him on the floor. He holds on to my calf as I lean over to Katie and give her the look, like *Stop this.*

She finally stops talking and starts to cry. "What am I going to do?" I hold her like I hold my children and gently rock her.

"We're going to get through this."

She is trying not to cry, and her face tightens as she groans, "I don't think I can."

"Shhh. Of course you can." She then fills me in on reality instead of make-believe. Jack went to the doctor for a lump in his neck that she found when they were making love. She tells me about the exams to come and the stages that will take place: x-rays, biopsy, meet the oncologist, decide the treatment, probably chemo. She looks so tired after she tells me the facts.

"I gotta go ..." she says when she's finished.

"Why don't you stay down here?"

"I can't," she says as she picks up her keys and purse. I can't stop her. She has already made it to the door by the time I reach down to pick up Cole. She gives me a brief hug and then she is gone. I turn off Baby Einstein and put on the Talking Heads "Burning Down the House"; it plays as I make a pot of hazelnut coffee. After taking my first sip, I start to pick up toys in the living room. Cole begins to get fussy and I take him upstairs for his nap.

I feel helpless; I want to call her on her cell, so I do, but she doesn't pick up. I have to do something, so I start cleaning. The caffeine has hit full blast. I decide to take over the room that used to be an office and sometimes an overflow guest room but has now turned into the dump-anything-in-it room. I pick up, and I mean I *really* pick up. I take the things that don't belong in the room and put them where they go, throw out things that should have been thrown out a long time ago, start a bag for Goodwill that soon turns into three bags. But right before I fill that third bag I crumble to my knees and cry for Jack and cry for Katie. I call her cell but she still doesn't answer.

Now I am obsessed. I organize the kids' drawings, knick-knacks that Alex brings home from school, and small art projects into a box that soon flows over with snippets of creative childhood. On a rainy day I will make a scrapbook, or maybe not. Maybe just a shoe box labeled "Kids' Stuff." I straighten furniture, clean, polish, vacuum and begin to redefine the room as a room—as mine. Cole is awake and at my feet, but I keep him entertained with trucks and other odds and ends that I find along the way. He is being so good; he is letting me get this project moving. I feel like I am accomplishing something, even though I also feel so helpless for Katie and Jack and their family.

Then after dinner, when the kids are in bed, I am at it again.

Blake comes in after I have placed scented candles in etched blue glass cups on the desk. I go to fetch a ceramic blue bowl from the kitchen as he sits on the now-cleared couch. I wish he wouldn't do that; I just cleared it off, and now he's smashing my down pillows. He's still there when I fill the bowl with oranges from our backyard and garnish it with leaves from the tree. I want to make a perfect arrangement in the center of the desk. *My* desk. He eyeballs the computer and goes to check his e-mail. He gets on my nerves. I wish he would get out of my space.

Blake begins to follow me. "Tate, are they okay?"

I stop, look straight at him, flowers from the yard in my right hand, and blurt out, "Can you believe he has cancer?" I want to crumble.

"No," he says with zero emotion, picking his teeth.

"I don't know what to do." I want Blake to come over and hug me, I want him to take away this pain, and he does for a second when he looks into my eyes and I see that he feels like I do. He asks, "Should I call him?" I had forgotten the two of them are friends, albeit more like friends of survival because Katie and I have been together so long. I want him to hug me ... maybe he wants me to make the first move.

"I don't know. I don't know anything anymore, not that I ever knew anything—"

"Ask Katie if I should call," he says, walking away. I could walk after him and grab his shoulder to turn him around, to him turn around so he can hold me, but I don't.

"Okay," I say as I place the flowers in sterling silver bud vases and set them on the small end tables that frame the cleared-off sofa. The pillows are fluffed where Blake smashed them flat. A few new pillows might give the room some accent—I'm thinking bright red and yellow, maybe even with my monogram in the center. Blake has gone upstairs. I could go up to talk to him, but I'm always the one who has to make the first move, so I don't bother.

I've opened the windows in my new room to let fresh air in. I burn sandalwood incense, which cleanses the air, transmutes it from stale and stagnant into something new, something that isn't so heavy and sad. I have already straightened the floor-to-ceiling bookshelves, getting rid of miscellaneous Matchbox cars, trucks, the boys' Transformers, a dirty pair of socks, an old apple core, and two mugs stained with coffee.

The over-the-top, y-chromosome books—how to restore your car, how to run a mile

under seven minutes, how to play no-handicap golf—were quickly taken off the bookshelves and placed in the family room. I then put every self-help and spiritual book that I owned in the newly empty space for easy access. These were the books I had forgotten about, like *A Course in Miracles*. The tattered old book was dusted off and used later to christen and bless my new room.

Who would have thought cancer would give me a room to myself? The office is no longer a dumping place—it's mine. Not only were the bookshelves cleaned, polished, and straightened, but pictures of me riding horses a lifetime ago were reframed and added to the nooks and crannies. A pair of old toe shoes was displayed on the fourth shelf from the top. My own knickknacks, found in the bottom of my bedroom closet, now reclaim the room, positioned as if on display in a museum that says, *Look in awe, but don't touch.* Like my favorite small Italian dessert plates that we never use but that I adore; like my favorite duck decoys, handed down to me by my grandfather, that are worth something. This room was prescribed by my therapist at the beginning of our sessions. *Find a room for you and only you, where you can rebuild your dreams and passions; a place to meditate, a place to renew.* But I never thought I could find a place to be by myself so that I could find my breath again—to find the hidden, invincible core that was once me. Katie had her room and had chosen to hide in it, not coming out so that I could comfort her. As she receded from me, I moved toward my own space.

I continued to work on the room for weeks, while Cole napped, when the boys were tucked in tight at night. It was becoming more than an office, more than a sanctuary: it had become mine. A room that no one paid attention to was quickly turned into a room that everyone wanted to be in. Was it the freshly painted walls? The French navy toile valances that matched the sofa perfectly? Was it the pillows covered with leftover fabric that perched on the restored leather chair behind the desk that made the room look designer-perfect? Gone were the days of abandoned school projects and toys that didn't work, unread newspapers, and cleaning supplies that hadn't made their way back to the laundry room.

I was told by my therapist that no one need come in and share this space. It was the *place to find my authentic self*— whatever that meant. It didn't need a sign that said *Do Not Enter.* The message was an unspoken rule, and if a child, large or small, stepped one toe onto the freshly vacuumed floor, there were consequences ... A look that could send them miles away. A looks that said, *I mean business.*

My therapist would have been proud. I created a boundary, and learned how good it feels to put myself first. And the truth is, it wasn't that hard once I made up my mind.

I burned a candle and scooped the light and brought my fingers to my face. It was like a Tai Chi dance, as if I were washing myself with the light. I lifted a prayer up into the air, sending love and healing to Katie and her family, and then asked, "How do I forgive?"

I open *A Course in Miracles,* with its worn blue cover and its fragile thin pages: *"Forgiveness Is the Key to Happiness" (Lesson 121): "The unforgiving mind is in despair, without the prospect of a future which can offer anything but more despair … It thinks it cannot change."*

Following the lesson was an exercise: Close your eyes. Place the person who needs forgiveness in front of you, and try to perceive some light in them—a little gleam that you had never noticed. Let the light expand until it covers that person, and make the picture beautiful and good. See that person as a friend instead of an enemy. *"Practice the exercise throughout the day."*

My mind is cloudy but I breathe deeply to dispel the mist. I sink lower and lower into the chair and hear my breath through my nose. I see my husband in front of me, and even though he bugs me, annoys me, I try. I try even though I don't want to be nice to him and it feels impossible to love him. I put a dab of white light in the middle of his chest and let it spread to his face until it is covering his entire body. He looks better now. He doesn't look as self-involved and unloving; he looks like an angel who I can begin to forgive. I open my eyes. Finally, I feel as if I did something right for myself.

Fourteen

"I am in need of nothing but the truth."

B lake and I got in another fight. He was overworked and sex starved. We were heading out for dinner on our weekly date night—a recommendation from the therapist. He was mad that I kept asking him if my outfit made me look fat and said, "If you think you're fat, you probably are. Don't ask me."

I wanted to smack him, then kill him.

But that wasn't the best part. The best part came when he ended the fight with, "If you come to me with a problem, expect me to give you a solution. That's what I do. Sympathy is for your girlfriends."

I now wanted to castrate rather than smack him. I was speechless, and it took a while before I could look at him without wanting to scratch his eyes out and pop his head off his neck. He had to apologize—which he did lamely.

"Honey, listen. I'm sorry. I'm tired."

He still got the death glare and the *Why should I forgive you?* look.

"Okay. Dad called me at work." I knew that expression on Blake's face. His dad didn't just call him, he called him up drunk.

"Yeah?"

"Yeah, whatever." He tries to flick it off like an insect on his shoulder. His secretary must have figured it out, because his face told me he was more embarrassed than usual.

"What happened?"

"I just told you," he says, agitated. He's not ready to spill the beans, he hasn't processed it yet for himself. He's still in denial of the things that really hurt him.

"He's fine, it's fine."

But it isn't fine and he is never willing to go there with me. Even with all this damn therapy, he doesn't go to the root of his problems, to the root of his pain. He is so slow to look at his own life. I let him off the hook by not pushing it, by not asking him more about it; his pain is still there. His hook cuts in deep to his soul, right through the belly, but he can still deny the anguish. He pretends that there is no hook at all.

Even though I thought I got over it, apparently I didn't, because the next day I practically ran up to Orange County to see Katie.

We are in her kitchen and she is pouring bottled water into a glass filled with ice and a thin slice of lemon. I notice her perfectly flat stomach and I casually look at my pooch from under the kitchen table. When she hands me my glass of water I realize I am sucking in my gut, but as soon as she turns around I push my chair in closer to the table and let it all hang out.

It's impossible for even a stranger to hate Katie because

of the way she looks at you—open and kind and without judgment. If I had her stomach I would judge the whole world and in my mind I would say things like, *Why doesn't she go on a diet* or *She could at least do a sit-up.*

"I can't stand my in-laws," I confide.

"I know."

"Why can't I just forgive these people? I used to like them, we used to get along," I say after a sip.

"That's when you used to like your husband. Now his flaws are glaring at you and you realize he's like his parents—he's a mirror of who they are and the mistakes they made."

"Really?" I have to think about that one. "But he doesn't drink. I mean, he's not an alcoholic."

"He doesn't have to drink to be like them."

"Does Jack ever tell you about the stuff that really bothers him, like the dysfunctional things? The scars of his childhood?"

"When we first dated." She is irritated with this question. She feels I want to talk about Jack and suspects that I'm using Blake to get to her husband's health.

She changes the subject. "Hey, let's do something different today."

"Okay."

"Put Cole in the stroller and let's do an affirmation walk."

"A what?"

"I don't know exactly what to call it, but I want to try out an idea."

"Okay."

But Cole doesn't want to go in the stroller; he wants to run. Cheerios, toys, and his favorite blankie don't do the trick; he is running around screeching. We play his game and run after him, I scoop him up and give him helicopter rides until my arms feel like breaking. He still doesn't want the stroller, so we resort to lollipops and two bouncy balls that he throws at us. Finally we distract him enough so we can talk.

"So, before we start, I think we should clear out all the crap in our heads," Katie begins.

"So you're going to perform a lobotomy first?"

"No. Listen, I'm gonna ask you some questions. I'm going to ask how you are feeling and walk you through a technique to move through heavy feelings."

"Excuse me, but shouldn't I be doing this for you? And shouldn't we be talking about something else?" She lets out a defeated mouthful of air and gives me a look like, *Can you give me a break?* which I answer with a *That's not going to work* face.

"Okay. He gets an IV of chemo in three-day cycles, then we wait eight days, then he does it again, then we wait two weeks, then again, and after that they check his blood count. He has been extra needy and the whole thing is overwhelming to me and the kids." She gives me an *enough already* look and then adds, "You can clear me after I clear you. I'm going to ask you questions, and even if you want to answer *no,* you just say *yes.* It's a way we can deprogram our minds; it's a way to force out the heaviness and allow the lightness to come in."

"I don't get it."

"Okay. What are you feeling now?"

"Confused."

"No, what is your *root* feeling? Take a deep breath and find the real feeling, the real emotion, the thing that is most heavy on your heart." I've put Cheerios and strawberries on Cole's stroller tray and have his blankie ready for his next fuss. "Okay." I breathe slowly, and then I breathe even more slowly. "I feel restless and anxious and ..."

"Good! Can you completely allow yourself to be with it?"

"Well, yeah, I'm with it all the time."

"Okay, now take a deep breath, and after I ask you these questions just say *yes* even if you want to say *no*. Are you completely willing to free yourself of this feeling?"

I take a deep breath. I am feeling even more anxious and don't know how to get rid of this feeling, but I do what she wants me to do because if I don't, she'll make me. "Yes," I say.

"Would you release this feeling?" She is looking straight into my eyes.

"Yes."

"When?"

I let go of a breath. "Right now." The chatter in my head begins to slow down and then stops. I start to feel better.

"What are you experiencing now?"

"I feel less anxious, better."

"Good. Now can you allow yourself to really feel this feeling?"

"But why? I feel better."

"Just stay with me, feel this feeling." I do. I let this little bit of restlessness fill my heart and wash over me and then she asks, "Can you let this feeling go?"

"Yes," I say reluctantly.

"Would you?"

The heaviness of this emotion makes its way up my throat and out of my mouth when I say, "Yes."

"When?"

"Now."

She waits a moment and then looks at my face. "How do you feel? Even better?"

I can't believe it, but I do. I almost feel like I'm walking in slow motion and that my surroundings have become brighter. We go back and forth with this little game of feeling our heavy feelings and releasing them into the wind until we do indeed feel lighter, maybe because we tell our minds to let go of what we were holding on to so tightly, maybe because God has shifted our thoughts. This strange little exercise releases the stresses in our hearts, our minds, and our souls. And surprisingly, Cole has relaxed with his blanket and started to doze. I smile at Katie and gently touch his head while I push the stroller.

"Okay, now let's start the real affirmation walk. This is how it works: there's no conversation; just say an affirmation, something you want to happen."

I know about affirmations. Katie has had me on an affirmation diet for years, writing them down on Post-it Notes and sticking them in places where I'll see them so I can set my mind straight. She tells me it's all about manifestation, all about the law of cause and effect.

She's really excited to do this, but I'm not so sure. "Okay," she says. "I'm first. My mind is at peace."

I say, "I get dinner ready tonight without stressing out."

She nods her head and smiles like that's it, that's good, and then continues, "My intuition grows greater and greater."

"I have stopped yelling at my kids."

"God's purpose for me washes through me and shows me that I am on course."

"My house is always clean— and when it's not I don't freak out."

"I am balanced, perfect, and whole."

"Cole's runny nose goes away and I don't need to schlep him to the doctor for antibiotics."

"My art heals those who view it."

"I have lost ten pounds without dieting."

"There is peace on earth."

"Blake and I stop blaming each other and arguing in front of the kids."

"My children awaken to their own spirituality."

"I never have to clean the kitty litter again." Now she's looking at me like I'm doing it wrong, like I'm not doing what I'm supposed to be doing.

She looks right in my eyes when she says, "My mind is one with God, my thoughts are clear and united with the Source."

This is where I slow down and think about what I really want to manifest.

"Jack is healed."

Katie's face tightens. "I am happy."

"I have begun to relax and let go of controlling."

"I am grateful for my many blessings."

"I'm okay with who I am even when I am around people who look so perfect."

"All is well in my world. I am safe."

"I have stopped worrying about the trivial."

"I am safe."

"I let go."

We continue like this for what seems a small eternity and I at times wonder if she is going to let up, but then all of a sudden we both magically have let go of everything we have ever wanted and we realize that we are full. Full of God and good and we feel whole. And in that moment something extraordinary happens: I feel calm. This crazy thing called an affirmation walk has affirmed that all is okay. I am calm. Katie is beaming, but the beam isn't too high or too strong, it's perfect.

We have made it back to her house. Cole is happy to get on the ground and move around. He heads for toys on a child-size chair. I pour water from a pitcher in her refrigerator.

"God, I feel great," she says.

"Me too."

"What's next?"

"I think we should create something together." I'm not sure where this idea comes from, but it feels right.

"Like what?"

"Like a book that empowers children ... Yeah, a book that tells a boy that it's okay to have all this wonderful power and energy inside of you and that it's okay to let it out with a hand that looks like a gun. Or a book that says it's okay to let your kids do stuff that drives you crazy, like get really dirty ... a book that says, *Celebrate who you are*." I can tell she doesn't like the gun idea.

She chimes in, "But it needs a parenting edge, like *Get off your cell phones, BlackBerry, and e-mail and be present for your children*. Children are competing with technology, and we aren't present for them. Let's face it, we're all guilty of using our cell phones when we shouldn't, like driving our kids around and talking about things that can wait. But kids can't wait, and we don't get that time back with them. It's lost." She wipes the sweat off her upper lip before she pats it with a cloth napkin.

"So your message is that parents should be connected and one with their children, living fully in the moment," I say, looking at her lip. "I get it, but how do you get that in a story?"

She looks out the kitchen window. "You go for the core—valuing the child's feelings in a compassionate and empathetic way."

I think her ideas are a little far-fetched. I suggest, "How about, don't freak out if your son wants to play with guns or swords. Think past the knee-jerk reaction and have a little bit of fun with what's going on—fall down when they try to kill you, play with their play. Show them all the ways to use the power within them and how to embrace that power, but more importantly, help them to distinguish between fantasy and reality. Help them feel in control when they don't feel in control, like in a divorce, or when their dog dies ..."

I ask her why she is so quiet.

"I'm building on a memory."

CHAPTER Fifteen

"This day I choose to spend in perfect peace."

There are no children in the yards today because it's raining. It rarely rains, but today it is pouring. The drops are big and fat and come in sideways, splashing through the few open window screens and leaving small puddles. The grey sky makes the outdoors one wet shadow; the bark of the trees is so wet that it almost looks black. The only thing that looks good through the bleak greyness of the day, through the thick low-hanging fog, is the green. The grass is so bright green, the leaves of the shrubs so full, so lush.

I love the way rain comes in softly and ancient. That it looms and drizzles a beat of mood that is somber and gives you an excuse to not be happy and that is okay within itself. It's like an off melody, not what is to be expected.

I close the window. I place my bright red, over-stuffed down booties on my feet and shuffle to my retreat in the study. Cole is napping. The daily ceremony begins. I strike a wooden match that breaks the silence of the room and light candles, saying a prayer as each is lit. Lavender is crumbled and smudged between my fingers to release its fragrance. I burn incense in a shallow bowl and wash the smoke over my body, like I'm washing away all the distractions, clearing my mind of all the unnecessary chatter.

I breathe. Slowly. Slower. Until I begin to feel calm. As I reach for my leather-bound journal, my cat comes in and sprawls on the couch. As quickly as the rain came, it leaves and things are still. I tap the keys on my laptop. I purge the list of things that need to be taken care of in the house and all the words that Blake has spoken that bother me.

Like the night before when I told Blake that Katie and I had an idea of writing books together. His response was, "Well, it better pay something. If you're going to take away time from the kids, you better bring in some income. I'm sick of supporting you."

He had the definition of support confused with that of devalue. I should give him a dictionary for his birthday. I had no idea he had become so angry. I thought it was a lack of sex thing, but my therapist explained that it's a lack of his own happiness. I try not to take his comment personally even though it crushes my new dreams, my heart, and my feelings.

The sun peaks out and the cat jumps down from the couch to the sunlight patch on the Oriental rug and immediately cleans herself with her scratchy pink tongue. Her slow movements mesmerize me. She has shifted my thoughts from sadness to peace, and I don't understand how my mood can change so suddenly. I write in my journal:

God, I can really see you today, clearly with no illusions. I see you through the sunbeams in this room, on my cat's fur that glistens so shiny through a shaft of light. I see you in objects in the room that look like artwork but are just or-dinary—the pillows, the furniture, my knickknacks. The air is still. The only movements: the sunray dancing and mov-ing the shadows across the rug. Everything looks so good. When I see the world through your eyes I am mesmerized by the beauty and grandeur of life. I am amazed that my large feelings soften to serenity—just for a moment, just for this moment.

This room was just a room, not something other than a grouping of three-dimensional objects, yet you make it look so beautiful, and why did I not see the room like this before? How did it change? I find myself saying thank you, thank you, thank you, wow, that is so beautiful, how come I didn't see that before?

I have learned to come in and out of my study when my life gets stiff or when I feel wobbly. When things do not flow and the light within turns murky. I close my eyes and open my mind in quiet meditation to stillness. I visualize different things—today, the Buddha, round and happy and full of compassion.

I am crying, although for what I do not know—maybe my marriage, maybe my fears. Behind the anger is grief, sorrow, sadness. In my mind's eye I place my hands in the Buddha's hands and sob. Sob the tears that blacken my soul. *Take away the pain so that I can be free of my own misery. Show me that this three-dimensional life is all an illusion. Show me the love.*

After dinner is cleared, I try to sneak into my haven to look at the light before it is gone. The light. Not a lot—a little. When dusk comes the shadows become long and the light is amber, warm, not bright white. Soft. Softens my insides again.

CHAPTER
Sixteen

"Forgiveness ends all suffering and loss."

The house is clean. Blake would be so pleased, and I can take Cole up to see Katie now. A clean house can do that—allow me to relax and go forward—because I won't feel him on my back. And it feels good to be with Cole now that he's in preschool a few mornings a week.

The sun feels good on my skin, warm, but a marine layer sinks in and makes everything cold in an instant. It's confusing because it's still bright, everything is still shiny. But the dampness of the air chills, so I grab a sweatshirt to get the cold out of my bones before I get into the car.

I thought my intuition was pretty good until I really started to use it. Then I doubted everything I was feeling because I was over-analyzing my intuitive radar. Instead of going right I go left. Maybe there is a sign from God on the left. Nope. Just a long way around to get where I was going. God, I gotta stop doing that.

Why does it take me so long to feel spiritually inspired or motivated or true to my purpose? There are times I think I'm on to something, that I feel *Wow, so this is why I'm on earth; wow, I really helped that person; wow, I am contributing to all of mankind*—like I get a single moment right. But the truth is those moments are fleeting. Most of the time I'm treading in my own waters of uncertainty.

When my mother painted landscapes she would squint her eyes; she said it helped her see things clearly, to see the lines of the shadows. If you squint your eyes and look at shadows in your backyard, for example, things seem more black and white than what was there before. I'm squinting, but I still can't see the light of my own insight.

So I've made a wrong turn again to Katie's home. I've only been there a million times. I thought I was taking a shortcut, but it turned into a long cut. Finally I am at her doorstep.

"Hey," she says low and melancholy.

"What's wrong?" I thought I was the one who was getting therapy today; I got that wrong.

"Nothing."

"Get out. Have you been crying?" Cole runs into the kitchen where the toys are.

"Nah," she says, inhaling leftover tear snot.

"What's going on?" I demand.

"He's gone."

"What?!"

"No, not dead. Back in the hospital—neutropenia or something."

"What does that mean?"

"Infection. He had a high fever, they say it's common—lack of white blood cells to fight off the infection. He gets antibiotics on a drip for four to five days. God, he's just so needy."

"He's got cancer," I say. My tone adds, *Give me a break. What's wrong with you?*

"I can't handle his being sick, he's just so pathetic. He's manifested this disease," she says self-righteously. I am stunned by her coldness. "All diseases, or dis-eases, are manifested by a weak mind and soul. In metaphysics all diseases are an emotional response to something in our lives that we have programmed into our minds. Cancer comes from a deep hurt, long-standing resentment, grief eating away at the self, carrying hatreds from the past. I keep telling him to read the Louise Hay book to reprogram his emotional response, but he won't."

"He's your husband!"

"Exactly—you'd think he would get it."

"What is wrong with you?"

"God, you don't get it either. I can't handle his being sick."

"Oh, I *get* that. Can you at least try?"

"This is none of your business; this isn't your life."

"Maybe we should change the subject."

"Grand idea."

She has built a fire in the fireplace. The bright colors of her living room become warm from the glow. In the center of the room is a square chest that must have belonged to Katie's grandfather. She has made it into a coffee table, and it houses stacks of old leather books, a wooden bowl filled with pinecones, and a robin's-egg-blue urn filled with birds-of-paradise and gerbera daisies from her garden. Next to the flowers she has placed a tray with an Oriental teapot, two handmade ceramic mugs, scones, homemade muffins and ramekins containing assorted jellies. Plus cut-up fruit and veggies for Cole in kid-friendly cups. *When does she have time to do this?*

I think. *I thought she was depressed and her husband had cancer.*

I stop being so judgmental. "How can I help you? How can I make you feel better?"

"You can't."

"Can you tell me again what happened?" I ask, as Cole pulls his way to my lap, pinching my skin 'til it hurts with his strong chubby fingers. He is making his way to an apple wedge and practically knocks my tea over, but my hands are faster and keep the accident from happening.

"He doesn't know how to forgive the past, so he has manifested cancer."

"What?" I say in a wisp of a voice. I realize I'm shaking my head; so much for not being judgmental.

She's crying. She's crying the ugly cry with her face all pruned up, mascara running, a slobbering cry. When Alex cries like this I feel helpless. I put my arm around her. Cole immediately grabs her calves, hugs tightly, and kisses her shins. Once she's stopped sobbing, he goes back to his Legos on the floor.

"Can you tell me anything more?"

"There's really not a lot more to tell. I dropped him off yesterday."

"Have you been staying at the hospital? Should you be there now?"

"No."

"God, he is the last person on this earth that I thought this could happen to."

"Yeah, well," she says sniffling, still prune faced. "Let's not talk about it. Let's talk about you."

I try to cheer her up, but forget about it. I'm too sad and shocked to do a good job.

We fumble around her house doing nothing until it's

time to go, and I still don't know what to say or do. My mind drifts to what my life would be like without my husband, or with my husband with cancer, and it makes me so sad. I want to be with him so badly for the first time in so long that I can't drive back to the house fast enough. Maybe I should give my marriage a chance.

CHAPTER Seventeen

"Conflicting wishes cannot be my will."

A couple days later, we are going to have the most amazing split pea soup ever, not because of the smoky, sweet flavors of the ham, not because only the finest ingredients have been added, but because Katie is in my kitchen, and anything she touches in my kitchen will become gold—something everyone will love, even a picky three-year-old.

I've taken the bone from the baked ham and cut off the succulent meat. The ham is perfect for split pea soup, not just because it's been slowly roasted over hickory chips, but because it's been slathered to perfection with brown sugar, honey and secret spices.

Homemade chicken stock is poured over the bone, and large bits and chunks of the ham are cut up and added. The peas have been soaked and cleaned; their once dehydrated bodies have come alive. Eight cloves of garlic and an entire white onion are minced and sautéed in butter and then thrown into the pot, along with carrots, celery and their leaves, fresh thyme, course salt and pepper and the secret ingredient—cumin.

Katie's kids are here too, and even though they are seven and nine years older than mine, they are having a good time running, kicking balls, and playing make-believe with the young ones. I watch them play, I relax, my heart swells. There is something about someone loving your kids as much as you do that just about knocks you out—it knocks me out cold. It's as if my love extends through my kids to Katie's kids and vice versa. The air is filled with laughter and I just about want to die I am so happy.

But then I remember why she and the kids are here. I remember why I get to have them for a sleepover, and my heart sinks. The kids are still coping with their daddy's cancer. He requested a weekend alone so that they wouldn't be around it all—all the stuff that comes with recovery.

Katie needed to get away from the house that has the clothes and sheets and towels that smell of him. It is a house filled with him, but she says he's not there. The kids feel it and struggle to form the words that can free them from the way that they are feeling, but no words come out. So she gets them out of their house and she brings them to mine—their second home, a safe harbor and a place that loves them unconditionally.

I look out the kitchen window at the sun low in the sky; it looks like melted copper. The shadows begin to lengthen in the backyard. I used to think there were no seasons in California, but that was before I learned to observe the subtleties. Autumn isn't colder, just cooler, than summer, without the acorns but with cloudless, deep blue skies.

"So how are you holding up?"

With a mischievous smile she says, "Great. There's this

great guy I met at the gallery who bought two of my paintings." She is blushing as if she just uttered words that she wants to swallow. Her smile is ill behaved, and I wonder if she is stepping over the line in playing with the idea of an affair. I want to ask her if she's lost her mind. I want to ask her if she has lost her soul—the one that used to have feelings. And then she answers for me.

"He's been asking me over to see how the art looks at his home."

I look at her frozen, my eyes stretched so wide that if they could speak they would be saying, *What?!*

"So I went and it looks great; his home overlooks the ocean." I want to say, *You've got to be kidding me. What the hell is wrong with you?!* but if I do she won't give me any more of the goods.

"Sounds nice."

Katie wants more. More than cleaning up a grown man's vomit without a thank you. More than having to deal with the heaviness that touches her children's hearts—it's all too much to bear. She thinks there is nothing wrong with having someone acknowledge a piece of her art that came from her soul. What's wrong with seeing the place where her art is viewed every day, adored every day? That's not so hard to understand. Who wouldn't want that when you're not appreciated at home?

"Tate?" Blake comes into the kitchen from the backyard. "Are we ready to eat?"

"Yep."

He goes back out to round them all up. Katie tries to take the towel that I've been using to clean the counters from my hands, but I'm holding on to it tightly because I want to slap her in the face with it. As she tugs she says, "Sorry, but can you be just a little less mad and a little more compassionate?"

I let go of the towel and offer, "You know, I have to believe that I had a hand in all this."

"What?"

"No, seriously. I might have wedged you two apart before all this, being so needy for your time and advice. He obviously needed you more."

She slams the knife down on the counter. "Oh, please. Just because you got your shit together and he's floundering, you don't have to blame yourself for his inadequacies." She watches to make sure the kids are not coming in yet. "You know over fifty percent of all marriages end in divorce; now I get it. I never thought I would ever understand it, but the truth is, none of us is safe from the unknown. I'm trying to be grateful the guy is alive, he loves his kids and loves me, even though he doesn't show it."

The kids are still making noises outside and she says quickly, "He's now on his own search for reality. I had mine, I get it." She looks me deep in the eyes. "Tate, it'll be okay. This kind of cancer, all the doctors reassure me, is very curable, especially because he's so young."

She goes to the window and looks out, her face filled with sadness—like she's trying to convince herself of what she just tried convincing me of.

She turns away from me, and her hair picks up the light. I go to her and pull her hair back softly. I lightly touch her back; there are no words to share. I know she is in that place that feels so heavy and consuming, overwhelming. Her hand reaches back for my hand, and I give her a hug and say, "Everything has a place for a miracle. Something good will come out of this mess." She turns around and smiles. I am so sad for her. I am so lonely for her. I am so helpless.

Eighteen

"I will not be afraid of love today."

The loud sounds of children being children bellow out of the Katie and Jack's home.

Katie's hands are square on her hips as she speaks in a mocking voice, "Boy, your kids are behaving so badly. Do they always fight like that? Shouldn't you be doing something?"

I laugh. "Yeah, right. If I showed you a film of what you were like as a kid, you'd be appalled!"

I have to remind her of the story she told me about a time her older brother bent over and dribbled a long strand of spit on her forehead while she was reading a book. She retaliated by making his cereal in the morning and spitting in it when he wasn't looking. Little did he know that his Grape Nuts had become a petri dish. Katie had a sore throat and, like magic, he was sick a few days later.

The events of Jack's cancer and treatment mean that I get

to see Katie more. We've had a slumber party every weekend going on a month; either she brings her kids down for a night, or I go up with, or sometimes without, mine. Blake was not happy.

He barked at me, "How much more are you going to dump on me? How much more do you think I can handle doing—I do everything!" He actually believes what he says. *When did he become such a baby?*

"Blake, it's just one night. I don't know why you're so upset. I'll do dinner and clean the dishes and put the kids to bed and then go up. All you're doing is having breakfast with the kids; I'll be home by lunch."

"I'm not doing it, Tate. I never get a break."

"Fine. We'll go up today—you can have the whole weekend."

I really hate him. I hate him so much. But the truth is, it's better without having to owe him. He always makes me feel so guilty when I go without the kids—which has been twice.

"Let's cook Thai tonight. Basil and mint are bursting in the garden, and I know where we can get lemongrass," Katie offers.

So we chop bite-size pieces of onion and pepper and mince garlic. There are about a million ingredients in Thai cooking, and all are imperative to create the layer upon layer of flavors. She cuts vegetables like a sushi chef, small and precise. The smell of mint is strong as she minces it; it's one of the secret ingredients in Thai food, she tells me, that and saffron. The way she sautés the vegetables is the same way she plays with a double strand of pearls. Elegant.

The only other person I know who cooks Thai is her husband. Jack uses a lot of coconut milk in his cooking, and it has to be fresh. He isn't the type to climb up a tree to retrieve coconuts; he's the type who would blast them down with a BB gun. He would say that wasn't a violent method, but strategic.

Jack hides in the bedroom or his office when we are there. When Katie checks the sticky rice, I slip in to see him. "Hi. How are you?" I'm looking for a soul answer, nothing glib. "I'm okay, Tate, thanks for asking." He's become so soft and nice. Why can't Katie see that? "Really, Jack, how are you?" *Hey, it's me, it's okay. I'm safe, you can tell me.* "You know, it's a journey and I'm humbled by it all the time. Cancer is a funny dance of gratitude." "Yeah."

His skin is so white and his eyes seem to be watery all the time. I'm not sure if he is crying or if that's just what happens when you get cancer.

I offer a meek, "Is there anything I can do to help you?" "No," he says with a smile and a soft shake of the head. He can tell I mean it. "There's really nothing. I just get so tired. I wish I didn't feel so wiped all the time. I feel like I'm sleeping non-stop when I'm not working." "It's a process—that'll pass." "Yeah, I guess. Thanks for helping with Katie. I know she couldn't get through all this without you." "I don't know about that." "No really, thanks Tate. I'll be there in a sec for dinner."

Pain does crazy things. Jack wouldn't tell me, but it made him look at things in his life that he never wanted to see—a bald head, vomiting at the office, voices from his past. He and Blake had more in common than they wanted to admit—bad fathers. Blake's father drank, Jack's father cheated. I couldn't understand how Katie could even consider having an affair, when that's the one thing that would bring the hidden pain back into his life. Life is funny that way. If you haven't fully healed the demons of your past, they'll come back with a vengeance to make sure that your healed muscle is fully developed.

Dinner at this house seems—even with Jack's cancer—so much more normal than at ours. They are so friendly with each other, moving dishes, helping the kids. Their actions and mannerisms are perfect—maybe too perfect.

The only thing my kids eat a lot of is the rice and the chicken satay on skewers, but they do eat—a lot. I realized the best way to get my kids to eat is let them watch older kids who like to eat. Out of admiration, they do the same, almost in a trancelike state.

Jack is mostly quiet at dinner but smiles like he is taking it all in. Soon after the dishes are cleared, he excuses himself to go upstairs.

Katie and I have become wine and martini connoisseurs, also known as late-night alcoholics, when the kids are in bed and not underfoot. When we are at my house, Blake joins us for one and then heads off to his home office to "get some work done." I think he just wants to escape our laughing and crying. We are too female for him, too emotional, too needy, and too feeling. It's just as well; we can't really be ourselves with him around, can't get to the good stuff. But Jack seems different now. I feel like he could hang with us if he wanted. It's obvious that Katie wouldn't like that. She can't clear him away fast enough.

Jack is asleep, just like all the kids. He sleeps a lot, like a newborn.

We've just stopped shaking Katie's father's silver monogrammed shaker full of vodka, triple sec, and cranberry. The drinks are garnished with lemon swirls and go down easily. I lick my finger and place it on the rim of the martini glass, sliding it around and around and wondering if it will make the high-pitched sound that comes from real crystal.

"Blake needs to go get fixed."

"Is that because you're mad at him or you don't want any more kids."

"Both."

"Why not put him on the male birth control pill?" she offers.

"Honey, he hasn't changed the oil in his car in a year. What makes you think he's going to remember to take a pill?"

"I can see Blake getting snipped," she says with her familiar pushed-out lip, nodding-head gesture.

"He says yes, but the real answer is no. I keep telling him it's just a day of frozen peas on the two bigger peas."

"You don't really say that, do you?"

"No." But I really did. "I think he won't do it for fear the doctor might sneeze."

"I wish I were a proctologist right now and Jack was my patient."

Man, did she just say that? I go to change the subject. "Do you think you could die from secondhand snoring?"

"No, just firsthand. Secondhand you're already in the spare bedroom." She takes a sip and the bright yellow rind sinks into the pink, icy liquid.

"I read today that speaking a foreign language makes you more attractive."

"Jack better become tri-lingual."

I try again. "Do you remember when people would fall into burnout at work?"

"You mean corporate America? The place where we got a paycheck with our name on it? The place where someone else made the coffee? The place where we didn't have to clean the bathrooms? The place where lunch was brought in? The place ..."

"When did you start missing your job?" I ask, surprised.

"I dunno. I miss the freedom."

"No, you've forgotten it's all the same"

She squints her eyes like she's saying, *What do you mean?*

"Do you remember when people started to feel burned out, they started to resent the company, and they became hostile. When people felt like there was nothing they could do to make things fair, they'd start to come in late, leave early, or steal office supplies—they justified it by saying that the company owed them. It was always a signal when procurement let me know that office supplies were disappearing; I knew morale was probably low."

"Yeah, so?"

"So, it's the same with us, but instead of the kids stealing office supplies, they fight more, or we fight with them, or they scream instead of talking."

"Yeah. And how did you turn things around at work?"

"I'd get my employees to keep their eye on the prize, encourage them to do their best, to stay the course. Like the promotion, pay raise, sales award was around the corner. There are two keys to helping make people successful at work. One, never take it personally when people aren't happy, and two, lead by example."

"And you're going where with this?"

"I think it might be a book idea."

"Kids getting promotions?"

"Well, maybe. Yeah."

"And they would be promoted to . . . ?" she asks.

"I haven't gotten there yet, but I think if we use terms

that the child and parent share, they'll both start feeling better—they'll both get healed."

She pushes her lower lip out and starts nodding her head, like, *I think you've got something here.*

I don't want her to get sullen again. "Me Jane. You who?"

"Huh?"

"You who?"

"Yoo-hoo?"

"No. You who?"

"Like the Hostess Cup Cake?"

"Never mind."

I tried again. "What else is there to say when there is nothing to say?"

"Nothing?"

Exactly!

She gulps down the rest of her Cosmopolitan. Her eyes seem foggy. The martini glass is in need of a refill, and she helps herself. "God, we are profound tonight!"

It is here in the midst of our bumpy lives, just as we are trying to get things back together again, that the Cosmos begin to go down too easily. The kids are deep asleep, like we should be, when I remember Kahlil. I am again running my finger along the rim of the glass, mesmerized by my own movements. I let my mind wander.

Sleep deprivation, kids, and a husband still have not taken away the pieces of *The Prophet.* I take a sip of my cocktail and savor it. I surprise myself when I start reciting:

"When love beckons to you, follow him,
Though his ways are hard and steep."

Katie looks at me strangely as I continue,

"Love one another, but make not a bond of love:
And stand together yet not too near together:
For the pillars of the temple stand apart,
   And the oak tree and the cypress grow not in each other's
shadow. "

"Where didth thhat come from?" she slurs.

"The miniscule part of my brain that still works."

"What does it mean?"

"Which part?"

"All of it."

"You're drunk. This stuff is right up your alley. It means everything it says."

"Say it again." Now she's focusing.

So I recite the pieces again, slowly, almost too slowly for someone who isn't smashed.

And she says, "That north wind has been in my garden, that's for sure. What would make you memorize that?"

"Because it pertains to all relationships. I love the idea of a relationship being like a Roman temple and not having the pillars too close or too far apart. That each person in the relationship is like the pillar, strong and individual. If the pillars are too far away, the temple is unstable. If the pillars are too close, it's not a temple but a fortress. You give someone space to be their own person ... Like us, we give each other a place to grow and be our own selves, and we have a strong temple."

"Are you asking me to marry you?"

"Honey, where have you been? We *are* married."

Nineteen

"I am never upset for the reason I think."

Palm trees, Torrey pines and a Japanese maple on oc-
casion, the land of fruits and nuts. I have so much to
share. I have so much that I want to say because I'm bursting with an epiphany. Thank God Katie is on her way down
to visit. We agreed that she would come over before I had
to pick up Cole from preschool.

"So how was your shrink appointment?" she says as she
puts her purse on the counter.

"Great." I place a yellow bowl full of chips and a smaller
bowl of dip on the table.

"Why?" she asks, helping me put out napkins and getting bottled water from the fridge.

"She said something very interesting. She said that my
anger was a good thing. Can you believe it? She actually
said my anger was a good thing and to embrace it, to be
thankful for it."

"Shut up!" She's being sarcastic because she's said the same thing to me. The difference is, when the shrink said it, I got it. Katie has scooped a ton of dip on a chip, and I'm thinking she could eat the whole bowl and not gain an ounce.

"I know, that was my first reaction. I'm thinking, *Are you crazy?* I tell her a million reasons why my anger is so bad, like that it scares my kids. And she says that *that* kind of anger is non-effective anger, or rage. But real anger is good. And I'm looking at her like, *Hello? Are you joking?* And she goes on to define anger as a tool that helps to set boundaries so you aren't a doormat. It was this amazing discussion of how it can be good. Good, actually good. It struck me square, *BAM*, right between my eyes."

"Yeah, and—" Katie says through her teeth, talking and crunching down on a chip at the same time.

"She told me stories of people who don't know how to be angry. They can't get angry, so they eat and get fat, or pop pills, or do other stuff. And I still don't get it and then she gives me the whopper analogy. She says, 'Picture yourself in a playground, and picture a five-year-old boy who is being spit on by a bully who calls the little boy names, kicks him, pushes him, and the little boy just stands there saying nothing—he can't or won't defend himself. Frozen.'"

"Man, she went for the jugular." Katie stands up to go to the fridge and takes out two more bottles of water and an orange.

"No kidding. That's when I got it. Could you imagine one of our kids suppressing their anger and being beaten up?"

"Yeah."

"Who?"

"Jack Jr.," she says, opening the water bottles.

"No way." Jack Jr. is the last child I would imagine suffering this type of victimization. He's an easygoing boy who is just like his father: beautiful, green-eyed and articulate. When he was smaller, he would sit in my lap like Cole. I've always thought he was the perfect child mentor for my boys.

"Yeah," Katie says. "But I'm working on it and it's getting better. It would be a lot easier if—" And then I know what she is going to say or wants to say; she wants to say it would be a lot easier if Jack weren't sick, so he could help with the kids. Help speak to them when they are so scared. Teach them to be strong and defend themselves. But she doesn't say anything, she's quiet. "I'm sorry, Tate, I didn't mean to interrupt."

"God, stop that! Your life is so big right now. How are they? How are you?" She shrugs like she's ignoring the questions. "Please go back to you. Please, it's so much easier right now to think of someone else's stuff. Tell me more about your therapist. Please?"

I'm quiet. I don't want to go on about my little stuff, I want her to talk.

She says *please* again. Now she is peeling an orange and separating the pieces.

So I sit down slowly and look at my hands. "Well, she takes me back to where the anger came from and, of course, we start talking about you-know-who."

She's quiet. I don't look over, because I feel her pain too much, because I hurt too much for her. I peek up. She's nodding her head to go on, and then her eyes drift out the window as she sucks down an orange wedge.

"I felt that I was powerless growing up under the cloud of my father's rage. You know all this; you know he wasn't an alcoholic like Blake's dad, but in some ways I wish he had been so I could understand why he was so mad all the time." I look at her and she is listening so intently. "Some-

116

thing shifted today, something really shifted. I am able to name the power my father holds over me and look at it and not be scared of it and actually see that it has *benefit*. It's like this was the thing that I couldn't stand about my father as a kid, and now I get it.

"I see where he was in his life, how he was raising us under so much pressure. I see him in the times he tried to watch over us when my mother was sick. He tried to support and take care of us all. And then his job that didn't work out on top of it, and he finally landed and stayed at a job that he didn't like. So what if my parents still have power over me, so what if I'm like them, so what if he can still make me feel like a kid. Get over it, I say to myself. The power is in my hands."

Then Katie is really quiet because she can apply what I'm saying to her own life. She is silent and I wait, letting my eyes go outside my kitchen window to the ceramic pots filled with plants and moss and earthy fungus growing at the bottom. The sun is bright in the sky, making the day look new. She still isn't responding, and I add one more thing: "I want to stop putting them at fault and being so angry. I might be repeating what I don't want to repeat. I want to give myself a chance to be the person I want to be."

She says nothing because it is too close to home, so I change the subject to her painting and what's going on at the gallery. I watch her; her words are few but fluid and move easily through her lips. "The gallery is fine—paintings are moving and then not moving."

I think of the NPR segment from that morning and offer a change of subject when she starts talking about how tired she is. "I heard somewhere that when men are looking for a dentist they should look for a woman. Pain seems less intense when it's administered by a woman."

She interrupts, "Unless she's your wife ..."

"True."

She looks straight at me. "What is it with marriage that makes things so hard? What is it that makes us *want* to be their dentist and drill a hole in their head?"

"Because it's the only way we can tell if there's anything inside?" I say with a smile, dip my finger in the dip, and lick it. "The process of marriage is this: I love you. You are perfect. Now change. Do they do that to us or do we do that to them?"

She's getting mad. "Maybe if the conversations didn't start with 'you just don't listen' we wouldn't want them to change. Did they *ever* listen?" She pushes her chair back and crosses her arms.

"Yes, when they were enamored."

"Did things start to change when they began to sprout body hair in the strangest places; their ears, noses and even their backs? Thank God for chemo—makes his skin tolerable. It's the unending whining I could do without," she says, without a smile to let me know she is joking.

I want to judge her right here for being so insensitive to Jack, but then I realize I would be insensitive to her. And then I realize this is the first time she has really seen life as not so perfect. "Nah. You can deal with the whining, it's those damn hairs you can't deal with."

"No, seriously. When we were dating and madly in love, if he gave me a copy of his favorite novel, or a mix tape of all his favorite songs, or let me wear his favorite sweater that smelled like him, I was goo-goo gah-gah. If he did that now I'd probably walk away and think, *Are you kidding, it's all about what you like. Where's the thing that I like?*"

I interrupt, "The guy doesn't have a chance. We think he's insensitive for showing us something of what he's made of, something that he's interested in."

She cuts in, "When's the last time Blake gave you a mix tape or made you breakfast in bed—?"

"I don't know—a long time ago," I say with a mouth full of nectarine.

"Case in point. See, the difference between men and women is this: If the girl says to the guy, 'You have an exceptionally small penis,' the guy gets drunk with his best buddies and whips it out for examination. They all tell him he is King Kong dong and he believes them. If the man told the woman that she had really small breasts, she would believe him. She might ask her therapist or girlfriends, but no matter what they'd say she'd still believe she had small breasts; she would feel deformed and broken."

"Oh come on, that's too harsh."

"Why?"

"You don't think men are sensitive?"

"No, not really."

"Wow." I look hard at her and realize she sounds like me, and it sounds so bad.

"I'm seeing things for what they really are without the illusions."

"Are you sure we're not in the illusion?" This is something she would say to me.

"No."

"Well, I think you could be."

"What?" she says, as if I have betrayed her, even though I'm dishing out her own medicine, her new-age medicine that I now take and like, but which is not working for her.

She's confused.

"Yeah, I think when you feel broken you get stuck in an illusion," I continue. These are almost the exact words she's given me from *A Course in Miracles*.

She scoffs, "Give me a break."

"I think that when you can't see beyond your own pain,

you start blaming the one who's closest to you. He doesn't understand his fear, his whining; his pain is a cry for help. You don't understand that he's crying out to you for help."

"But *he's* the reason I'm feeling this way."

"Yeah, I know what that feels like, but I think you're wrong now and were right before."

"Come again?"

"You used to believe that love was what was real and what is not love is an illusion. Wait here."

I run to my office to get the worn blue book off my desk. I leaf through as I walk back to the kitchen, and then I find it. She is brooding when I say, *"Lesson 51—I am never upset for the reason I think. I am never upset for the reason I think because I am constantly trying to justify my thoughts. I am constantly trying to make them true. I make all things my enemies, so that my anger is justified and my attacks are warranted. I have realized how much I have misused everything I see by assigning this role to it. I have done this to defend a thought system that has hurt me, and that I no longer want. I am willing to let go."* I close the book, look straight into her eyes, and say, "What do you think?"

And then there is a flicker behind her eyes. I see the glimpse of light that is the glimpse of God, and then it is gone.

"When did you go soft?"

"Now. The same time you became hard ... What do you think men are most afraid of?"

"Going bald and having a bad hair-transplant, the kind that sprouts hair out of the plugs that are an inch apart," she says, making things light.

"No, really?"

She rolls her eyes. "Not making enough money...okay, okay...cancer...not finding their purpose in life."

"Nope."

She's annoyed. "All right then, what?"

"They are afraid that they won't be loved. When they don't look good they won't be desirable and loved, that they have lost their breath, their passion. Sound familiar?"

"No, not at all!"

"We're not so different. Pillars of a temple look the same, are the same."

"Whatever."

"Okay, on that note of forgiveness I gotta get off the rag here and pick up Cole. I wanna get some writing done later on."

"So you're kicking me out."

"Of course not, you can hang."

She's pissed. She wants to wallow in her pain, and I want her out of my house and on to someone who will mope with her. She's not ready to have someone give her own medicine back to her, and I don't feel like a pity party.

As she walks out the front door she says, "Nice planted pot. Who did that?"

She taught me about self-love and now has forgotten it for herself. I found I had more energy when I gave to myself first. She's forgotten because she had a real crisis in her life, things weren't sailing so easily. But were they ever? The more time I spent in my sanctuary of peace, prayers, meditation, and quiet, the more patience I had with my kids.

"We did." Meaning the boys and me.

I had collected pots from flea markets, garage sales, and gardening stores. Once I had the lot of them, I would take out one at a time from the garage and make a special project with the boys. They loved the dirt, getting their hands brown from the soil, squeezing it, pinching it, throwing it, and getting it thick under their tiny fingernails. Boys, dirt, and fresh air are a good mix.

One pot at a time was doable, so that's all we did. The expectations were low and manageable. Each pot became its own magic garden—and each had a theme, like "Pirate Plants to Mark Gold," the green sprouting leaves in the shape of an X. "Dragon Mint for Dragon Breath," "Flowers That Scare Away Monsters," "Evergreen and Ivy for Wizard Brew." One was made of moss and dwarfed trees: "Hobbits for Humanity." We even made a labyrinth with trails of sand and crushed rock that the boys could run their Matchbox cars over.

The recipe for success, I found, was just doing one thing with the boys and doing it well.

This was a key to bringing happiness in and out of the house. The thing about California is that you can have plants that bloom plentiful all year round, and you can have fresh-cut flowers in a vase every day of the year for pennies.

Twenty

"There is another way of looking at the world."

Blake is starting to look hot. How did that happen? He looks amazing: a great pair of old faded jeans, a white button-down shirt, a navy blazer, no socks, and worn loafers. The best part about him is that he doesn't mind wearing color, like his bright yellow flannel pullover, or his red sweater and his pink oxford. Or even an orange polo with khakis. He's like a human scoop of sherbet. American classic preppy.

I can look at him now. I mean I can look at him now and see that he is still handsome and that he hasn't lost his youth and his subtle glamour, and that still makes me think, *Wow, he is really handsome. And I'm with this guy?* It's his eyes, those eyes, so blue, framed with fine-lined wrinkles that give him wisdom, making his appearance soft.

It's date night and he's taking me to Giovanni's Bistro, the best Italian gourmet around. We sit in the back patio under a ficus tree illuminated by tiny white lights that swirl around the massive base of the tree and spread out to the main arteries. The air is cool but not cold. The smell of garlic is deliciously thick.

We have a small table with a view of the wall fountain—a lion's head thick with green algae giving it a patina effect. The water pours out of the lion's mouth into a basin shaped like a shell, which then overflows to a pool of orange and white carp—elegant. A baby mourning dove flies and sits on a branch above the tables next to us and I'm thinking. *Shouldn't that dove be sleeping? Isn't it too late for him to be out? Where is his mother and why isn't that bird tucked in bed!*

The waiter comes to fill our glasses with our favorite Cab and we take our first sip and let out a breath that says, *Aah, no kids—peace.* We are relaxed and we look at each other as if to say, *This wasn't hard. Why did it take so long to get here?*

He lets me rehash the day and the week's events that I hadn't had time to fill him in on. He is interested and listening while our entrees come.

I am still talking and he interrupts me. "Tate. Tate. What are you doing? I can do that."

I realize I am cutting up his fillet.

"Oh God, sorry." I was on autopilot … gotta stop that.

"I ran into Kate today in LA."

"Yeah?"

He says like he has discovered foul play, "She was with another guy."

"What?" I say, almost spitting my wine in his face.

"It looked strange—"

I interrupt, "How long were you going to wait to tell me?"

"I just saw her four hours ago. I needed to unwind first—"

I interrupt again, "My God, don't do that! Tell me every-thing."

If Blake decided to have an affair or move out and not tell me why or not make contact with me, the day he stepped a foot back in the house he better hope that I'd become declawed.

"What was she doing in LA?"

He is chewing his food so slowly, and I'm thinking, *If he would just let me cut smaller bites he could get to the story faster.* He finally washes his steak down with a sip of wine, clears his throat and then tells me the facts.

Katie has become a Rembrandt painting gone bad.

Twenty-One

"Let me remember what my purpose is."

After speeding all the way to Orange County with thoughts of killing my best friend, I have finally made it to her kitchen and am ready to unload, but I can't get a word in.

She's talking and talking and won't shut up. She's flitting around, putting dishes away. Her words come out too quickly to interrupt. I need to say something. I need to unleash. But she won't come up for air. She's going on and on like an untied balloon releasing all its air as it deflates into a small crumpled shape. She's going on and on about nothing. I try to stop her—intersect her speech with an "Ah ..." or a "Hey ..." and even a "Wha ...," but nothing works. Her dribble cannot be broken.

"Would you shut the fuck up!" She is stunned, a bullet straight through her heart. She doesn't have to say, *What? Where is this coming from?* She can't, because the wound is deep and motionless. I swore at her—the CARDINAL SIN—the thing that she hates most. I should say *Sorry* right there, right then, but I don't. I'm pissed and on fire and my temper is going to flair out of control, like it's unfortunately done before.

"Why can't you stop talking and just listen for one second!"

Her face is red, redder than mine, not from anger but from anguish, as if I've spattered her own blood on her cheeks.

"I listen all the time to you," she retorts with a pissed tone.

"Yeah, like when my mother died. You were there listening to my every thought, right?" Now the gun is to her head. Now she can't talk even if she tried.

"It's funny; when the big stuff happens, you vanish!" She knows what I'm talking about. I'm talking about our past, and I don't need to give her the specifics. Now the buried pain is going to roll right out.

"I couldn't be there when it happened," she nearly whispers.

"Because?"

"I ... I ... I don't have that ... I can't ... I don't know."

She doesn't fight back—she doesn't even try. She can't because I'm going to unload and let out all the demons that live in our friendship, all the things that I've hated from the day I met her. It's not going to hit her like an avalanche; it's going to hit her like death.

"What is going on with you? What is really going on with you?!" I practically scream.

"What do you mean?" she's a bad liar.

"Where the fuck were you yesterday, and with whom?"

"I don't know."

"Liar!"

"I don't know."

"You fucking liar. You know what I'm talking about. You fucking liar, who is he!?"

She can't breathe because she's crying so hard, she's heaving and bent over and sobbing, sobbing. She looks limp and helpless. But I'm not buying it; I'm not here to be nice and hold her hand.

"What the fuck is wrong with you! Why do you have to pretend that things have to be so perfect, so smooth—so in denial. How long were you going to play this game?"

She says nothing.

"You made up this big elaborate lie—a guy who bought your paintings? What is that all about?"

"He did."

"Yeah, right. Blake saw him. He wasn't buying any pictures in LA!"

"You just don't get it, Tate."

"Oh yeah, *I'm* the problem. How long did you think you could keep this a secret? God, Katie, what the fuck is wrong with you—you have kids!" I'm so mad I want to kick her, kick some sense into her.

She fires a round at me. "I think you like wallowing in your misery and your anger; I think you find it enjoyable. You don't know how to hold your emotions in check."

"What? Why would you say that?" She's made a clear hit.

"Because you choose it."

"Wha ... what? I don't choose it—sometimes I'm just, just ..." She's wounded me.

"No, you've chosen it." Silence. Now I'm crushed. "You're always so amped out. Have you ever been content?" She's sucking me into her game.

"Yes. You?"

"Maybe."

"What are you doing?" I don't want to be talking about this.

"When? When were you content?" She's relentless, her face focused on mine like a nuclear warhead.

But I've taken a breath to try to become patient—I can play this game. "The list is a mile long. Where should I start?"

"Name one. One time you were content."

I try to stop spinning so I can prove that she is so wrong. "Okay. The day I first learned to ride a horse, my first day en pointe in ballet, playing tennis with my older brother, graduating college, when I got a job after every interview ... the day I got married. The births of my children, when my kids wrapped their arms around me for the first time and told me they loved me, every vacation I took as a child—"

"Those where only moments."

"That's what being content is. Sewing all the moments together and embracing them like one continuous event."

"And you do that?" she says, arms crossed.

"I try to embrace all my moments, even the irrational, large ones." Now I ask her the question I have wanted to ask for years. "Hey, why didn't you talk to me when my mom died? Why didn't you ever call me back?"

"I couldn't."

"And how do you think I felt?"

"Bad."

Silence.

"I had a feeling, but I still wanted you to," I say quietly.

"I'm not made like you."

I want to talk about that time; I want to open the can of worms, even though it hurts like hell. "There was a reason we didn't talk to each other for that long—"

"Yes. You have strengths where I don't."

"Uh-huh." I'm still mad at her, I'm not going to take the compliment. I want her back talking about Jack and her kids and this guy, but she won't go there easily. "What's the deal with you and Jack?"

It was hard to imagine Katie wanted to have an affair. She couldn't have been looking for it. Maybe it started off innocently. He was interested in buying her paintings, maybe the interest in her came later.

He could have drawn her in—made her feel larger than life when he looked into her eyes, like he really saw her— saw her soul, appreciated her beauty. That same beauty that was taken for granted by Jack—ignored was more like it. Wasted—her beauty was wasted on Jack.

Jack only wanted her for *his* needs and his recovery from pain and fear. He had no time for her needs. I bet Mr. Gallery Man had time for her. Maybe she was tortured not because she had a strand of moral fiber, but because she knew it would break the fiber of her family.

It could have been that when he touched her body, it melted into his—that love chemistry thing that comes from newness, not the old stale marriage touch. Maybe they touched, they kissed, they petted, but they didn't have sex. But I bet she thought about it. She thought about it a lot—it probably consumed her. But she knew that would be a place of no return. She couldn't rationalize that it was only her body that wanted him, like men can do. Maybe she wanted all of him and wanted him to want all of her too. Who knows, I probably had it all wrong.

It's quiet for what feels like an eternity before she finally talks and tells me she has been seeing this guy but nothing has happened. I don't believe her.

She tells me when Jack isn't so needy he is wrapped up in his work. And I'm thinking, *He's probably trying to get caught up on his work so that he doesn't lose his job that supports his useless wife and her horrible habits.* She tells me she didn't know what to say or what to do for close to a month, so she confided in this man. And I'm thinking, *Thanks a lot, pal. Am I that invisible?* Okay, well maybe she has a point.

"God, poor Jack," I whisper. She knows I am thinking, *How could she be such a monster?*

"He's pushed all of us out—he doesn't want the kids in close to his pain and healing." She says this, but I wonder what the truth really is. It all seems so strange, so dysfunctional—dysfunctional even for her.

Then she takes a deep breath and says slowly, "Everyone deals with things the best way they can and the best way for them." I believe that but I don't believe her. But how and why would she leave me in the dark and play this elaborate game of deceit? I call her on it, But she gives me a lame, "I did my best."

She wants to shift the mood, shift the intensity of it all. She wants to connect with me because we are torn so far apart.

"You've got to get help, this is all so wrong," I tell her, defeated.

"I know," she says as she leads me out to her back patio and signals me over to the Jacuzzi. But I'm not ready yet to be friends, so I look at her from behind and still hate her.

She sits on the side of the Jacuzzi close to the small waterfall and dips her toes into the warm water. Her feet move slowly back and forth as her rigid body begins to relax. She turns her head towards me and gives me a face that says she is really sorry and *I wish I could explain, but I don't understand it either.* So I step near her, but I don't put my feet in the water. I still hate her. I still hate her a lot.

Her feet move slowly and ripples appear around her legs. She wears her hair up and I can see tiny blue veins in her neck, the neck that I want to strangle. Then I think of pushing her in and holding her down in the water to drown. I think I am strong enough to do that.

She looks up at me before I can perform my death act and gives me a childish smile that makes me take a step back.

After a long patch of silence she says, looking square in my eyes, "Picture that we have met a long time ago, before space and time. Maybe on a different planet. We're in a far-away place resting in a field of tall grass or maybe wheat. It's soft to lie down and wind blows each reed, bending the field like water. The rhythm of the wheat is tranquil, and we're laughing and laughing. There is no language; there is no division of space and time. It's as if we're on a plane where the three-dimensional means nothing. There's no sense of time because we are living in eternity. And then you look at me laughing and smiling and the sun or suns shine brightly on your face and I say, 'Wouldn't it be fun to go to earth for a thousand lifetimes.' And you smile back and say, 'Sure.'"

Goose bumps run down my arms. I rub at them, trying to make them go away. I don't even really believe in reincarnation, but this story is too oddly familiar. She continues, "I've had this vision, this image since I was a kid, but I never knew the person was you 'til I met you. It's been reoccurring in my mind ever since."

She dips her fingertips into the water and asks, "So, what are you going to do now?"

"Now? What?"

"Now that the thousand lifetimes are over?"

"Can you stop changing the subject and tell me what is really going on with you and Jack?"

I am still thinking about what she has just said, and I know I don't have to ask, *You think I've been here a thousand lifetimes?* I don't have to ask her because it feels as if I have. I have known this place that she talks about oh too familiarly—as if I have indeed been here a thousand lifetimes. She still says nothing about Jack, so I follow her bait, hoping to get her back on track.

I blurt out, "I'm done with this planet. When this lifetime is over, I am *so* out of here. Eternity, look out baby, 'cause I am coming! What about you?"

"I think I'll stay a little longer."

"What, are you nuts!"

"No, I think I have more to do."

"Well, you got that right."

She laughs.

She softened my anger and confusion to that place where friendship lives in unconditional love—well, partially. And in what seems a tiny instant I am free. I'm free of hating her and wanting nothing to do with her, and I suddenly feel gratitude that we're still friends. Something liberated me as she told me her dream. It's the truth of the story, or the idea that I can finally go home after this lifetime.

Twenty-Two

"When I am healed I am not healed alone."

The next morning I smell Blake's pillow and it smells sour. He doesn't smell young anymore. His sweat is no longer sweet with a light masculine musk; it's old and strong. It seems too early for the old man smell; maybe he just forgot to take a shower. I roll out of bed and roll into the daily task of restraining myself from being a psycho.

I finally enjoy my house when everyone is out of it and I am what is left. Quiet. I light a thick, scented candle that smells like gardenias and place it on the kitchen counter after saying a prayer of thanks. Outside the kitchen window, the grass is still wet from the morning dew and looks so fresh and lush and green and soft, like a newborn kitten. I wish I were a horse because that grass looks *so* good. I imagine the first bite, like the first bite of birthday cake or the first sip of coffee in the morning.

I walk to the living room and sit at the bench at the

piano. Throughout my childhood, the familiar sounds of my mother playing the piano filled our home. We, her children, were convinced that she could have been a famous concert pianist; it was only her modesty that confined her to this audience of three. We had a black baby grand Steinway in our first home, often draped in blankets to make forts to hide and play in as my mother played Chopin, Bach, Mozart, and Rachmaninoff.

Music does strange things, like preserve time or make a backdrop to the things that were good and precious, like etching them in stone so that they never leave your memory. Like how my mother's hands looked as they rested on the keys, or the sound of her laugh.

The sounds, the eternal rhythm that filled our home and filled my heart, have been carried into my home. As a child, I stank at piano. I think I only lasted a couple of months in lessons before my mother was nice enough to let me off the hook, probably to save her own ears. But a haunting memory that would not sleep, along with urging from my therapist to "try something new in your life and reclaim your old passions," made me take piano lessons many years since my childhood, even though I felt like I was too old.

At the beginning I was motivated and excited to fill my home with the sounds that I grew up with, to pass on the torch that lit my soul. The biggest difference was that instead of complex pieces by Beethoven or Bach, *Mary Had a Little Lamb* and *She'll Be Comin' 'Round the Mountain* were barreling through the living room, heavily laden with wrong notes. Something was lost in the translation; it wasn't quite the home I grew up in. But there was hope and there was time.

I was *much* older than the eight-year olds that my teacher usually taught, but certainly not dead. After four months of weekly lessons, a very patient piano teacher, a woman used to working miracles on eight-year-olds, made a miracle out of me. And before I knew it, I was playing Bach and Mozart and complex pieces by George Winston, and all at once I realized the compelling dream of passing on the tradition of my mother; she is still not forgotten. She echoes in our house with the stroke of each key.

The phone rings. It's Katie. It has been four days since our fight in her kitchen.

"Hey."

"Oh, we're talking now?" I say, half meaning it.

"We never stopped. Tell me your observation of the day."

I push through the feelings of confused anger I still have toward her and look out the window of the living room to the sagebrush and an old melalueca. It looks shaggy to the untrained eye, but to the native it looks lush and green and full of fragrance. "Guys don't want to be average; they want to be special," I say.

"Well, who wants to be average?"

"A below-average and unhappy person."

"So what other male observations have you made?" Her voice is so soft and nice.

"A real young buck, a ripe, virile man, is at the gym working on his Adonis body and he's thinking, *I don't like working out in front of women. I don't want them to see me when I'm on the way to the goal—which is them.*"

"Are you always thinking about men?"

"No, just thinking of people in general—men, women, we all think the same, at the core, at the core of our neuroses and our hearts. I need subjects that both kids and parents would be helped by for this book of ours, and I was at the gym this morning, and men are always there, and it got me thinking." By telling her this I am letting her off the hook from my anger toward her in a single moment.

"Okay, I got it. Tell me about the children's book part."

"I think the story should be about the key to eternal happiness: if you want to be happy, the first thing you have to do is be happy. For the parent, it's about approaching goals from a position of contentment, which gives you power that won't fade away. Live your life as if you have already achieved your goals. When you are desiring and craving, longing for that goal, the result is the intention. For the child, it's all about living in the moment without the restrictions of their parents. The book would bring it all together."

"How long is this book going to be?"

"Listen, I'm just brainstorming. Here's an idea: The child always wants a new toy, the next piece of candy; he's looking for happiness outside of himself. So it's the parents' job to change this, or at least be a catalyst for change. Right? The parents guide him like a wizard and make all the toys look brand new at home by just playing with them in a different way, by making the day-to-day look fresh."

Two sparrows and one mourning dove eat birdseed from the feeder in the backyard as I sink into a kitchen chair. I spy on them as I run my fingers over the bridge of my nose, feeling that bump in the center, feeling that bump in the center of my nose again, and then my hand heads for a piece of hair to twist.

The birds' movements are jerky. The seeds fall from the feeder, covering the bushes and the ground below. Then the birds are gone, scared by something that I don't see. My eyes search for the culprit, and all I can see in a patch of dirt a few feet away is a lizard the size of my husband's hand, chunky and fat, maybe pregnant, on a flat, round rock.

"Have you come up with words that the child will be able to relate to?"

"I'm still working on a concept line: Appreciate life today! Right now. How it is. Wish to be yourself and do it flawlessly." I'm masking what I want to tell her—I'm making up the whole children's book in the moment.

"Are you sure this isn't a parenting book?"

"It's a parenting book in the guise of a children's book."

"So how am I supposed to illustrate this?" I can feel Katie losing some patience.

"Listen, I'm just brainstorming here; it's only one day's work. But I'm clear on this: We need to create something that heals us, that makes us happy, and go from there. 'When one is healed, we are not healed alone.'"

"Where's that from?" Katie asks.

"*A Course in Miracles.*"

"Wow, how did you know?"

I say nothing. But I want to say, *How did you forget?*

"So have you outlined anything? Have you started to write?"

Then I think, *Why is she asking me this?* I know what she does before she starts painting. She gets out the dried sage leaves and burns them like incense and lets the smoke fill the air—a spiritual ritual that the Native Americans call smudging.

"No. First I thought I'd do a Shaman smudge," I answer. "Clear out all the negative cobwebs in my mind, because I've been feeling like, *God made me like this. Was it His desire, or His joke? Too many flaws.*" I'm basically making up fiction; I want her to talk about *her* flaws—I don't care about the book.

"Oh come on." She picks up on my vibes.

"No, really."

"No. I meant, when do you ever do a Shaman clearing?" she asks.

"All the time."

"Do you burn sage?"

"Of course."

"Really?"

"Okay, okay, this is a first. Why? Are you afraid that if I smudge to clear out all my negativity I'd singe my eyebrows and burn my hair because the burn of the flame would be so large?"

She says joking back, "Maybe just light a candle."

Finally I say what I want to say: "Hey, one thing—have you found a therapist yet?"

"Okay, gotta go," she says in a tone of *Buzz off, back off, and give me a break* and hangs up.

She didn't need me to tell her to get a therapist—that was her job. She was the one people go to for advice; she really didn't want anyone else's—like mine. I wondered what it was like to have a little danger with a man who was mysterious and handsome and doting. Maybe it gave her distressing life some spice and made her feel young. So skirting around the issue probably felt right—pushing back from my scrutinizing, judgmental eye.

I hung up the phone and walked back to the piano. I think I'll give it another try, to be like my mother—forgiving and perfect. I want to be a good friend to make my mother proud.

CHAPTER

Twenty-Three

"A happy outcome to all things is sure."

It's spring and the orange blossoms are in full bloom, exuding the scent of floral sweetness. The days are noticeably longer and it begins to feel like summer; the afternoon heat makes the days feel like they are in slow motion. The light at the playground is brighter.

Our neighborhood park has a nice playground with many jungle gyms, swings, and an oversized sandbox—more like a sand field that lies like a carpet under the main play area.

Cole buries his toes in the sand like an earthworm. His hair, like his father's—blond and shiny—blows easily in the breeze. He is so serious when he digs; unhurried and precise, trying to not let even one grain of sand spill. But he's still small and still new at this, so clumps of sand do fall from his unstable hand.

I know my head could easily clear from the day-to-day clutter when sitting next to him, if only I didn't have to think every second about his safety, his happiness, his well-being, Alex's well-being, book writing, *what's for dinner,* ...

Black ants are smothering a dropped Cheerio three feet away from me on the sidewalk. My butt bones dig into the pavement as my legs rest in the sand, my arms propping me up. I lift my chin to the sun that warms my face—that warms my son's head.

A playgroup of moms comes with their tots in tow. They are an arm's length away, almost invading my personal space bubble. They look over at Cole and me as if they are sizing me up or gently asking me to move out of *their* space. Some are slathering sunscreen on their children, struggling, squirming and screeching to be set free. Others set up camp, getting out lunch boxes filled with healthy snacks and taking out bottled water to hydrate their moving children. I am sitting close to them but feel separate at the same time.

As they are sizing me up, I am sizing them up too. I watch the mother who speaks baby talk to her three-year-old—must be her first born. Then I watch another mom who is too hands-off; her little Damian child is about to bite the arm off a baby. Then there is another mother whom I instantly like. She is relaxed and seems so calm, like she's really having fun, like she has been waiting for this moment to arrive. I like her and I like her cute outfit; casual and hip. I watch her, but don't stalk—a passive observation. Her outfit reminds me of something Katie would have worn in college.

Cole starts flinging sand at me, and I laugh as he wakes me up from my daydream. The cool mom is now to my right; her daughter has started to dig next to Cole.

"I like your shoes," she says.

"Thanks. TJ Maxx," I say, barely lifting my eyes off of Cole's chubby calves.

"Really?"

I nod.

"Do you guys come here a lot?" she asks.

"We live close by."

And in seconds, Ann and I are friends; the chemistry is perfect and we are laughing. Her playgroup is not so pleased. Not only are we both getting the eye of judgment, the neurotic mom, who has put forty layers of sunscreen on her child, looks over at Cole's bottom where his diaper is sticking out around his back and whispers to me too loudly, "Oh, he's *still* not potty trained?"

I want to poke her eyes out and then throw sand in her face, but I catch myself and say, "I know, can you believe it?"

Mrs. Neurosis dishes out the unsolicited advice that I wasn't looking for—doing the competition mom thing: *My child is better than your child and I am a better mom than you,* and *How fast can I make you feel small?* Mothers' competitions can be found at any playground and most playgroups.

It was time to go home. Ann and I are going to meet two days from now and try it again, *sans* her playgroup. As I pick Cole up, I smell his head, warm from the sun, fragrant with the recognizable little boy head smell. He wants to get down and run. Boys like to run, need to run and play—to let their legs feel long and allow their feet to touch the ground, soft or hard but rarely gingerly.

After lunch, as we head to his room for a nap, we pass the built-in cabinet that stores overflow towels and sheets. This built-in has enough space to do a one-thousand-piece jigsaw puzzle. It's in the upstairs hall, outside the boys' bathroom. The flat surface is never clear because it is cluttered with picture frames, so you couldn't actually *do* a jigsaw puzzle, but at least there is the potential. There's a picture of Blake and me smiling, wearing leis on our honeymoon. And a picture of me winning Grand Champion at a horse show. This is evidence that there was life before kids, before Blake.

I pick up a picture of Blake and me on a motorboat when we were dating, taken by the boat's captain. I faintly hear *"Mommy has a little baby, there he is fast asleep ..."* coming from the CD player in the study. I look at the picture intensely, only inches from my nose. *God, I was young.* My complexion clear and perfect, my smile one of sheer bliss. Blake is looking out to sea, content in the moment. I set it down and am taken back to that day. But I am reminded of the here and now by Cole's crying that he wants me to read a book to him.

When Cole is asleep, I go down to the kitchen to clean up. I am content in my movements, as if it's not a chore to get the kitchen cleaned but more of a ritual to make things fresh and new. I will go to my study to write—my newfound purpose on top of the other purpose: being a mom. Writing is supposed to give me purpose, but it often just makes me wonder whether it's my purpose or just another thing to do. The last counter is wiped clean before my eyes make it to the digital clock on the stove.

The clock reads 1:11 and I think it's a sign from God that I am on track. *I am one, I am one, I am one,* I think to myself. And I am one with the kids, and one with my family and one with the universe. The triple one comes back to me the next day, when I'm picking up Alex at school. Cole is singing his ABCs and it's a good moment as I look at the dash and it says I've driven 111 miles so far on this tank of gas. And I think, *I am one with Cole, one with Alex, one with God.*

And in these moments of contentment I begin to open up to more possibilities—like the possibility of a new friendship with Ann.

CHAPTER
Twenty-Four

"I seek a future different from the past."

My husband—great sometimes, pure male pain in the ass the other times. I was in a good mood when I awoke, but that changed when I rolled over and saw him.

My husband moves through his morning slowly, acting as if we were invisible except for when he needs something. Insensitive, but he can't help it—it's his genetic makeup. When it comes to doing something outside of going to work or briefly saying good night to his kids, he forgets things like—me. It's the details, like our anniversary or my birthday—well, sometimes he thinks of it. He can't be bothered with the minutia—like putting together one of our kids' birthday parties, or packing the kids' suitcases or backpacks, remembering all the things that *they have to have* before they walk out the door.

What is it with having to ask him to do something, anything, just one little damn thing while I am juggling several?

He's not blind or deaf or dumb—well, I'll get back to you on that last one.

Case in point—Cole. Cole is trying to go to the potty all by himself, and no one wants this more than I do—even without the scrutinizing mothers I don't know.

I am in the kitchen getting breakfast on the table, putting lunches in backpacks, and helping Alex finish a school project before we make it out the door. My teeth are not brushed, my stomach is growling because I'm hungry—but food won't hit the lining of my stomach for hours, there's no time for that now.

Cole is in plain view of Blake. Blake is scratching his balls, thinking about what he's going to wear that day to work. He stands in the hallway, stretches his arms over his head and lets out a big yawn; he has two ties in each hand and says, "Honey, which tie looks better?"

Cole is crying—he has just fallen into the toilet. Blake is steps away from Cole when he yells down the stairs, "Hey, honey, which tie?"

I dry my hands off, tell Alex to stay focused on the project, run upstairs, point to the better tie and clean Cole's tiny wet butt.

It doesn't occur to Blake to help with anything that morning—after all, it's the busiest time of the day, it's loud, needy and hectic, and he wants only to head away from it so that he can have some peace in his car and then have all his *people* stroke him for his ideas at work. He forgets that people love you when you're the boss so they can keep their jobs. I wish my kids had that same motivation.

Blake doesn't mean to be unhelpful when I need it most. It's a genetic, physical, mental, man thing—he's retarded. He can't help it, he's just made that way. It doesn't mean that he's cruel, or a bad guy, or stupid; it's just who he is.

So once again he wonders, *Why doesn't she put out, and why is she so angry all the time?* even though the therapist has told him why. But he still doesn't get it—he is a slow learner.

But this time I do something different. I don't yell at the kids when they're fighting for a toy after the dishes are put in the dishwasher. I don't give Blake an evil eye or say, "Can you help out a little?" because that will start the arguments spiraling. Nope. I go into the bathroom, shut and lock the door, and say a million prayers for mercy. I focus on my breath and do the exercises my therapist and best friend have told me to do to feel my power. I envision a light in the middle of my chest, like liquid love that spreads through my heart and out of my body and out into infinity. This light is like a lightning rod from God and it grows and spreads into my mind and quiets it, keeping my thoughts still, and then spreads through the fibers of my soul and begins to protect me from my racing thoughts.

This bright light is what builds me up—I don't feel so small. It's what saves me from feeling like a victim. It works—a little.

But there is one thing certain—signs of a shift. When I get out of the bathroom, like a biblical miracle in front of my face, I watch Blake putting Alex's sweatshirt into his backpack. The boys are no longer fighting—they have their father's attention. Blake makes animal noises and scoops them in his arms and spins them around like a helicopter.

Who is this stranger in my house? And where did this nice man come from?

He puts the boys down, kisses me on the lips and looks straight into my soul. "See honey, I'm trainable."

"I guess so."

It's funny; if he hadn't done that, I might have flipped

him off behind his back when he and the kids weren't looking. Or I would have said inside my head, *Have a nice day at work—retard.*

Things in my life started to fit, like the way my tongue fits in my mouth. Natural.

Once the kids are dropped off, I'm back at the house, taking in the quiet. I'm supposed to be productive. The book: write, get a new story, e-mail the list of agents. But instead of being happy about Blake's help, I feel wedged in my immobile fat body and not changed by my husband's changed behavior.

My sweatpants are tight on my tummy, so I push them down and let my roll of fat hang out in plain view. I squeeze it hard between my hands, compressing it on the sides. I press the fat flesh and watch my belly button turn into a crease; now you see it, now you don't. Squash, squish, now you see it, now you don't. God, that's a lot of fat. The Ben & Jerry's was a bad idea—again.

I walk towards the couch, heave my mass of dead, depressed weight onto the pillows, and flop. Flop. Flop and flail. Now I pinch the wiggle wobble under my arm. I hold up my arm loosely and flick at the skin that jiggles. Wow. I never noticed that much fat there before.

As I sit up, my eyes look down to my stomach; I squeeze the flesh through my T-shirt, swing my legs around, and head for the computer. *Maybe I should make some tea instead of writing.*

The phone rings.

Thank God. I push the talk button. "Hello."

"What's up?" Katie asks.

"Nothing." I'm tired of fighting from not being depressed—from being in limbo. She's there for me again.

"So you're feeling stuck?" *How does she do that?*

"Huh?"

"Try an affirmation," she offers.

"I suck."

"Come on."

"No. I don't want to. I am in this thing, this place of life that is—real. Would you let me be with it!"

"Yeah." Then she lets out a breath and something shifts, she is yielding. "There's a place in marriage when you want to give up, when you want to throw in the towel and divorce doesn't seem like a possibility. It's this place where you say to yourself, *I don't like this person, I actually hate this person and I want nothing to do with him.* But here is the epiphany—all men have baggage, all marriages have baggage, and then the question comes, *Do I want to deal with this one or find a new one?* At least with this one I know what his suitcases look like. So I've decided to take a year of patience before I divorce him and try not to say all the horrible things I want to say and ride it out with the help of a good therapist to see if I can get to the other side. It's like I've been sinking in this pool of uncertainty and hoping I would find the bottom so I could push off to get to the top— to the place where there is air so I can breathe again."

"Wow, where did that come from?" I say in shock.

"My truth. I see it every now and then."

"I guess so."

"Since you weren't going to admit that about your marriage, I decided to admit it about mine."

"Yeah, well, someone had to do it."

"Finally, we're in sync."

"Well, worse things have happened."

In this moment where I get her and get myself, my funk has passed over like clouds in the sky.

She has helped me even though I felt unhelpable. But more importantly, she is going to get help. She adds to this revelation, like she's reading my mind again, "Artists' blocks are normal. We are all channels of God, and the creative process will flow when we just show up. Just show up at the page."

When we hang up I feel present. Not spinning, not wanting, but present in my life and in the moment. I take in the surroundings of my office, my sanctuary, and take in the light inside the room. My eyes move down to the floor.

My cat is in a sunbeam, curled in an O shape with her chin exposed—her chin is up to catch a ray. Dogs do that too, lie on their back with the underbelly of their head showing as if they're saying, *Go ahead and scratch my chin, give it a soft rub, I won't mind.*

And when I am done stroking the soft fur of her chin, like after rubbing the Buddha's belly, I am healed and I can write again. Maybe a book about a pet that heals a child. And then the real story comes, the story about children using their infinite power to do incredible feats, and then another, and another.

CHAPTER Twenty-Five

"I judge all things as I would have them be."

The strangest thing on the planet happened. The eighth wonder of the world. I realized I had a social life outside of Katie—with Ann from the playground. Besides that awful playgroup that she was connected with, Ann happened to be connected to some very popular moms at Alex's school. I hadn't put it together—I was too caught up in Alex's classroom to get to know the kids and moms in the classroom a year ahead of his.

Who would have thought that she would show up in my life again for a girl's night out?

I don't know what it is about the beautiful, popular mommies. Wasn't high school over? Why on earth was I so eager to get into the graces of these women when there was no such thing as the popular group anymore … or was there?

What was it that put me under their spell? With a bat of their perfectly mascaraed eyelashes, I was a goner, stuttering when I talked, saying the stupidest things ever. As if I never graduated college, or went to grad school, or was a corporate executive who used to do amazing things.

Every time I was around them, I just felt bad about myself—fatter, stupider, more poorly dressed—frump, dumb mom. Was it their firm, fit, single-digit-sized bodies? Their fresh and flawless faces? I was mesmerized by how good they looked in clothes and the way they moved and smiled and waved—with that aloof wave.

For God's sake, I am a full-grown woman. Why did it feel like their eyes and questions were x-ray machines examining me, scanning me, exposing me? It was the strangest thing; in one breath they could build me up, but their next would invariably knock me down.

One day, when it was pickup time at school for Alex, I heard, "Oh, Tate, where did you get that adorable blouse?" Before I could answer, another pretty face chimed in with, "Did you get those at Neiman's?" pointing at my shoes. The answer was, *No, I got them at Marshalls.* Did she see me shopping there? I was stunned; I didn't want to answer. Luckily I didn't have to. I was being beckoned by Ann from behind them.

"Tate?" says Ann, waving in the background.

"Me?" I ask, looking over my shoulder and behind me to make sure she was actually talking to me.

"Hey there," she says, scooting in front of the belles of the ball and gently moving me aside. "Do you have a minute?"

"Yeah," I say, walking with her toward the classrooms with Cole in tow.

"Would you be up for getting out one night for drinks or dinner?"

"Sure." We are out of eavesdropping range by the other

women. They have gone back to their superficial talk of nothingness.

In an upbeat and friendly voice she says, "I could really use a girls' night out. I know the owner of this new restaurant that just opened up."

"When were you thinking?" Cole sees Alex and runs toward him.

"How about Thursday?" she asks while pushing a piece of paper with her number on it into my hand.

"Yeah, that could work," I say while looking at her perfect handwriting—she must have gone to a private school.

"Call me and we'll settle the details."

"Sounds good," I say, stuffing the paper into my pants pocket.

She told me the place was casual and the food was great, but I instinctively knew she would be a little dressed up. At our second playdate, like the first time I met her, she was well put together—unlike me.

Blake came home early and was surprisingly supportive of my outing on a school night.

Finally I could dust off one of my navy blazers and put on a pair of shoes that demanded respect instead of ready-set-save-your-child sneakers. I spent over an hour getting ready for my big night out—an eternity in the world that I ran in.

When I showed up to the restaurant, my eyes told me my instinct was off: she *was* casual, and I wanted to sprint back home and change. She wore jeans and a trendy blouse, which provided a major contrast to my triple-strand, Jackie O pearls.

Ann came towards me, opening with, "Oh Tate, I'm so sorry. I should have told you it was casual." She did, but I didn't listen. Meeting new friends is kind of like dating without the going-to-bed part. I wanted her to feel at ease with me and like me, and I was hoping to like her too.

Before I left the house, my boys were so excited for my night out. They watched every move I made to get ready for the evening, telling me over and over, "Oh, Mommy, you look so beautiful. Mommy, your hair is so pretty—can I touch your necklace?"

I began to relax and unwind after my first sip of wine. The converted beach cottage was warm and trendy with its yellow walls and oil paintings of fruit. I knew this place was going to be a huge success, not because of its casual and comfortable feel or its impeccable service, but because every dish that came out of the kitchen oozed with love and care.

"Thanks, Tate, for doing this. I really needed a break," she says, taking a bite of fried calamari.

"Tell me about it," I say, while watching her eat most of the calamari—I love her appetite.

"I've been looking forward to spending more time with you. You always seem so calm and peaceful." *God, did I have her fooled.* "Yeah, right.".

"No, seriously. You have a way of making people feel at ease—comfortable."

"Do you need to borrow some money?"

She laughs. "Stop."

And in seconds we are laughing and telling our life stories—where we grew up, life before kids, life now—in full sentences that are not interrupted by our children. If anyone was making anyone comfortable it was Ann. I could see why so many people liked her. I liked her for lots of things; she was warm and grounded, she kept her natural hair color, she had a quick wit—*and* she ordered dessert.

"How would you describe men?" I ask.

"Left-brained, driven to engage and conquer without

thinking about the consequences." *Something that I might say.* I add, "Yeah, their left brains help them to create legacies, but not with disciplining their children."

Then she asks, "Do all men struggle to make money, or do they constantly think about the struggle to make money?"

I could have judged her right then and there, and wondered whether her husband worried about money. Did he struggle? Not wanting to sink to the competition-mom level, I let her off the hook with, "Both. Women are the ones who help them with these struggles, nurture the children and set normal priorities, trying to put their lives in balance."

Then she adds, "Yeah, women help them focus on their big bright visions and we help them look at the bigger picture of their controlled, tightly restricted worlds. They can't tell us when we're screwing up, but we tell them all the time."

Now we're getting personal, and I wonder if we are going too far, but I didn't care, so I add, "If men are so good at playing games, then we're good at keeping score."

Without saying a word she toasts my glass, like saying, *Amen to that,* like saying, *I like you, we think alike.*

After my second glass of wine I talked too loudly and spilled a little of my drink when I talked. She laughed at my jokes, which were really just observations.

We ordered a hot chocolate lava cake with two spoons. My movements were sloppy from the third glass of wine, and as I looked down to my silk blouse I noticed it had drips of chocolate. Ann's eyes met mine and she asked, "Where's your bib, honey?" We laughed so hard I thought I'd pee my pants.

Strange things come in stranger packages. Who would have thought I could have so much fun with someone other than Katie?

CHAPTER
Twenty-Six

"I gladly make the "sacrifice" of fear."

In my therapist's office, I feel on edge: we are about to make a breakthrough. And it's been my experience that in order to have a breakthrough, you have to hit the wall first and dig up all the feelings that create emotional charge. Creeping around the wall of denial, stubbornness, and blame, or living on the surface without deep connection, was not making new strides in my life. Not to mention making me feel miserable.

"Blake doesn't support me," I blurt out, and before I start dumping out all the things that bother me about Blake, my therapist interrupts and says, "Blake, would you be okay if Tate and I spoke alone for a moment?" Blake gives her a look like *Thank God! You mean I can really get out of here? Thanks for the hall pass!*

After he has shut the door and headed for the magazines in her lobby, she starts coaching me. "Tate, tell me why you think Blake doesn't support you." So I give her the list and she gently interrupts me to ask, "Why do you think he doesn't support you?"

"Because he can't. And I don't think he has the capacity to. But I try to forgive him and accept him for who he is. But it still bothers me." I say the forgiving part, but don't really mean it.

She continues, "The advantage of thinking like that is that you feel safe in knowing that you can live your life like it is. But how do you know that he can't be supportive if you don't let him try?"

I think about that and say nothing.

She adds, "It's been my experience that instead of telling a man what you *don't like* and what you *don't want*, you should tell him what you *do want* by pumping him up." She goes on to explain that men think and act differently than women, and in order to get acknowledgment and support *from* them you have to give it *to* them. At first it sounds a bit far-fetched.

"Can you think of anything that he *does* support you on?"

My first thought is no. But then I take a moment and come up with, "He gives me Saturdays off and he financially supports us."

"You need to acknowledge him every time he does something right. And when he doesn't do something right, you don't react or say anything, even though it is human nature. Walk away and sit on it. You take the time to let the steam roll off and you tell him like this, 'It makes me happy when you do this...' and then you tell him what you need and want."

She is looking at me for a response; I want to say *That won't work,* but I know if I say that, I won't be making progress toward finding a solution to my stuck marriage.

She smiles softly when she says, "Just like you would with your children, you acknowledge him for every act of loving kindness. And trust me, when you slow down and look for those acts, you will be surprised with what you find. He's a good guy, Tate." There was a time when if she had said that, I would have thought her a traitor. Now I realize she is right.

I know she's right but I don't want to do it and she sees it on my face.

So she tells me a story about a couple that's finishing therapy with her and how the husband is always telling his sixty-year-old wife how beautiful she is. And the way she tells the story, you instantly love the husband. She tells me I can acknowledge Blake for his good looks, and she gives me other suggestions on how I can tell him what I want by telling him in essence the things that I want to hear. But the catch is—I have to be sincere and it has to come from my heart.

It was a session of hard homework, but not Mission Impossible. A data log: a few minutes each day of *practicing supporting my partner.* Each day I was to list one behavior where I noticed he was supporting me, and he was to do the same. She said that three to five minutes a day, every day, would change our lives. Like flossing—a small daily task that would have life-altering results.

After she was done coaching me, she had a ten-minute one-on-one session with Blake, and then brought us both together to explain what this was all about.

"I know you may think that this small daily exercise may not be worth it, but it is the stepping stone to changing your core beliefs." She went on to explain that Blake and I had the same *core belief*—we felt unsupported by one another.

And in order to change this core belief, we had to change behaviors, which would in turn change the feeling of lack of support and acknowledgment, which would then change the core belief.

And when our time was up, Blake and I left the office and rode an empty elevator down to the main lobby together. He was surprisingly calm and almost looked relieved. I was dying to hear what he said about me when *I* was out of her office reading magazines in her lobby. So I pried, "Well, how was it when I left?"

"Fine."

"Well, what did you tell her?"

He was looking at the buttons inside the elevator when he answered. "You heard her. She said she wanted to discuss that at our next visit."

"Oh, so you threw me under the bus."

"No," he said and meant it.

Wow. I felt bad because I sure didn't say nice things about him. Maybe she was right, maybe he wasn't such a bad guy after all.

"Blake." The elevator door was about to open. "Thanks for going to therapy. I really do appreciate it." And I meant it.

He sees it in my eyes and answers with a smile, "You're welcome." He says it so warmly and he is being so kind that once we make it outside into the parking lot and in front of his car I touch his elbow softly and look straight at him and say, "Can I give you a hug?"

"Sure." His body is stiff when my arms are first around him, but then he succumbs and hugs me back lovingly.

CHAPTER
Twenty-Seven

"Forgiveness lets me know that minds are joined."

Here's the pat on the butt.

I'm in the kitchen making dinner when Blake comes in from work. He looks tired as he gives me a peck on the cheek. "When your book gets published, let's go out to the opera and a night on the town."

"What?"

"Yeah, let's live life large and different." I turn around to look at him; he has already loosened his tie and is now unbuttoning his top button.

"Have you ever gone to the opera?" I ask him.

"No, that's my point."

"Okay," I say, confused.

"I was also thinking maybe we should consider taking the boys to a dude ranch, or go camping, or both. Live a week or two on the plains." He says this while dipping his finger into the red sauce and then licking it.

"Are you experiencing a testosterone leak?"

"Tate, I'm serious. We do the same thing over and over as if we're seventy-year-olds trapped at the same old bridge game. I say we mix it up a little. More oregano."

I thought he was kidding. All talk and no action—until a month later when we're off for ten days in Wyoming. On the big open plains, to a dude ranch for a summer break. I didn't think places like that existed. Stuck in time or created to look stuck—old and primitive and simple. It was my own personal plan to become a female horse whisperer before the trip was over, or at least be admired by a Robert Redford look-alike. That didn't happen.

But what did happen was that the boys, husband included, sat around the campfire at sundown, which turned into a night of looking for shooting stars and pretending to eat baked beans and have a farting contest. But the pretending became reality and the farts stank and then there was the flying farting contests, and face farts, and then the smelliest—you get the picture. Bed never came too soon.

Boys and animals are a good combination, like fresh air and blue sky. If riding horses and doing farm chores doesn't wear out a child, it at least places a permanent smile on his face. Less is more. The smell of the land, the soil and hay in the sunshine, it was all good. Clean fun without being clean.

There is something about no televisions, no computers, no cell phones. There is something about living a day with not looking at your watch to see what time it is, but looking at where the sun is in the sky. Time takes its own rhythm and your body seems to coincide. There is nothing like being so physically exhausted that when your head hits the pillow, sleep is immediate.

I didn't know what was better, having our kids touch a

teat of a cow to milk it for the first time, or having them run around the ranch catching frogs and fireflies at night. The air was better, the stars were brighter. The sky was bluer than I'd ever imagined. I forgot about the smell of a campfire and how the smell stays in your hair and it's a good thing. I forgot how good a hot shower feels after your legs are so sore from riding a horse for too long. But the thing I forgot most, the thing I love most, is the smell of the barn— horses and the smell of their breath. Heaven.

Blake found his heaven again, too, and it was only a small trip away. He took me out of my home, and I found home again right inside my heart, bursting.

Wyoming was the first of our off-beat trips. Trips where we didn't feel guilty for not seeing our parents and doing the whole extended family thing. These were the trips for us. The things that we would want to do for ourselves if the others didn't exist. But we all did exist, making it better to share the love of our own adventure.

In the mountains, if we weren't riding, we were hiking. I could feel the bones of the landscape under my feet. Squirrels came out of their hiding places, and sometimes there were tracks that you could imagine belonged to deer or moose.

Nature naturally brought us back to center. Nature can do that. Free therapy.

Blake was one of those rare male birds who was now grounded in the part of his life that wasn't related to work— the place that is usually man's toughest challenge. I was drawn back to the optimism of Blake's independence, his solitude, the place where no one was let in—until now.

CHAPTER
Twenty-Eight

"I am affected only by my thoughts."

Back home, life as usual—underslept and picking up dirty socks, soiled clothes, bowls with oatmeal and raisins stuck to the side and no dishwasher or laundry detergent.

My little blue-eyed boy is not so cute; he threw a toy at me as I brought in the groceries. It's a metal airplane the size of a Matchbox car and it hits my face half an inch from my left eye. My eyes water as I drop the brown paper bags and look at him in shock. He sees that he has hurt me and now kicks the bag of groceries on the floor. "What's going on?" I ask, picking up the groceries so he doesn't do it again.

"I want my red car!"

"Why did you throw the airplane?" I ask, feeling to see if my face is bleeding.

"I want my red car!" he screams as loud as he can, face red, fists clenched.

"Then get it," I say, heading for the bathroom to see if my Ralph Lauren modeling career is over. No blood, but a red puffy pillow. He has followed me into the bathroom; I lean down to talk to him, but he interrupts.

"You get my car!" Now he kicks my shin and I spin around wanting to yell at him. But I remember my latest parenting class and I try to stay calm and push out the thoughts of doing something I will regret. I look at him at eye level and say, "What's wrong?" My voice is calm, even though my face stings and my shin has a bruise forming.

"I want my red car!"

So I try to take his hand to find it, but he pulls away and then crosses his arms and stomps his feet—he's not going to budge. So I walk into his room and bring him his car, which he hurls right at me. I duck and want to hurl it back, but instead I take a deep breath and try to get close to him. But now he is kicking and screaming—he's in a full-fledged, ugly blowout tantrum. Nothing I try to do comforts him or makes him stop—not the gentle pleas, not quietly walking away.

Now I am upset. I try to ignore him as I put away the cold groceries, but he starts to kick chairs and then he heads for my sanctuary—my office—and I spin around before he starts smashing my favorite things. In the moment it takes to put the eggs and butter away, I realize, *Oh, he's tired, it's nap time,* and instead of taking something away from him that he likes, threatening him, trying to put him in a time-out, screaming at him or just plain fighting with him, I scoop him up, legs and arms flailing.

His small chubby hands pull my hair hard, ripping out a little fistful of strands. But I know if I lose it, it will only make things worse. So I breathe and pray. I get him to his room, I grab his blankie and I put him down softly. His face is beet red and sweaty, and tears are streaming down his cheeks and nose. His foot makes contact with my shin— hard, same spot as before. He turns around and is out of his bed; I scoop him up and rock him and gently blow on his hot sweaty head, but he smashes my lips and tries to tear them off with his amazingly strong tiny hand.

I try to let my feelings of hurt go—I detach from what he has done and is doing to me, and I see him as a small child and not the monster that he would look like to anyone but his mother. I relax and I breathe and I rock him, knowing that sleep is not too far away—hoping it's not too far away. And then, in what seems like an eternity but is only a second later, he's asleep and I wonder how I could have been mad at such a precious thing. His face is like an angel, and in that moment I am so grateful that I did the right thing, that I didn't lose it or do something that would have caused me guilt, but instead pushed through it and found peace. I got that moment right.

I go back to the kitchen to finish putting the rest of the groceries away when my eye catches a movement outside the window— a hummingbird taking the nectar of a ruby red flower. Bougainvillea. I am mesmerized by its spinning wings, how it simply floats on air—so perfect. The hummingbirds in my backyard never go for my hummingbird feeder; they always poke their long beaks in a real flower, never the red rubber flower of my blue glass feeder. It's probably because I never change the water as much as I should, or maybe because I put too much or too little sugar in it. Maybe ... the phone rings.

"I'm on my way down." It's Katie, panicked.

"Uh, okay. Where are you?" I say, cleaning off the countertops.

"Thirty minutes away. Didn't you get my voice mail?"

"No, I was ..." Her phone breaks up before I can answer and then goes dead. So I listen to her voice mail, which says, "We need to work on our books and get something really done."

She arrives twenty minutes later and I have all my notes, publishing resources, and laptop waiting for her in the kitchen. Cole may be up from his nap around an hour from when she arrives. She seems more agitated than she was on the phone, but she's trying to hide it by setting the table with snacks that she has brought with her—fresh fruit salad, baby quiche, gourmet crackers.

Katie is putting down place mats and cloth napkins when she says, "I just read an article on how difficult it is to get published."

"Fear—that's the other person's problem," I say before sipping on the tea that was just brewed.

"When did your theme become carnage?"

"We can do this," I say, blowing into my cup.

"I'm not so sure."

"Just hang on and watch." The truth is, I wasn't as confident as I came across to Katie. I was trying to convince myself that it would all be okay. Maybe, just maybe, we could beat the odds.

Her voice has an edge, like, *Come on, we're losing time,* when she says, "So, what *is* this book going to be about?"

"Well, here, check out some of these notes." I share with her the story lines that I had been working on, character sketches, research on what sells, and what's hot in the children's market, and just as we're going to get started and actually do something, Cole comes in from his nap. He's is not the grumpy child of two hours ago—he's soft and cuddly.

"Oh, great," she says, exasperated. But then she catches herself and recovers with, "Hey, Cole."

He picks up her vibe, because even though he loves her, he ignores her and climbs up into my lap. His face is puffy with sleep.

"Well, how much work are we going to get done now?" she says.

I laugh.

"What?" she says.

"It's funny. Motherhood is getting in the way of our book on children and motherhood."

She doesn't get the joke. She is too tense, too stressed.

"This is not like you; what's going on, Katie?"

"I want to get this book done!"

"I get it. I get it. But is there anything else you want to talk about first?"

"No, Tate. Stay focused. What am I supposed to illustrate with all this?"

"Lighten up," I say playfully and pick up one of my "how to write" books as Cole climbs down to get something in his room. "Here, check this out, 'The creative process should be fun and organic—'"

She interrupts, "What does that have to do with the story?"

"You of all people should know that you can't be tense when you do your art. You're the one who has told me, 'My best paintings are when I'm playing with my art and things just flow.'"

She slows down to take this in by letting out an exaggerated exhale. We really should be talking about Jack so she can unload and relax. But that's not going to happen.

In walks Cole with his worn, ragged, well-loved blankie. He now climbs into Katie's lap; she kisses the top of his head. He looks up to her and asks, "Auntie Katie, you draw me my blanket?"

So she pulls out a turquoise pen from her purse and starts to doodle. Then Cole takes the pen gently and tries to draw himself on top of the blanket, and like a flash of light Katie and I stare right at each other, jaws gaping. We read each other's minds when she says, "That's it!"

And in a second we are doodling with Cole and the words spark into my head and I begin to write. We fuel ourselves with coffee. The analyzing has stopped, the pushing too hard to create something has stopped, and we begin to play. And in that playing comes joy, and in that joy comes the outline and structure of the story along with a handful of sketched illustrations. We accomplish in an hour and a half what we had been trying to do for months.

Writing the book was a process, and all the pieces counted, like the research and the discipline of sitting down every day and trying to make it come together. But things really began to happen when we got out of the way and let the divine energy flow—through play and joy.

CHAPTER
Twenty-Nine

"Only an instant does this world endure."

Once the book was finished, it was time to get published. Katie was no help, offering, "Tate, you're the business genius. I really can't help you with that part."

It doesn't take a genius to do work—it only takes time. Something that I had little of and something she had more of. But having her help with the query letters, phone calls, and submissions would just make more work for me, so I forged forward and ignored her endless questioning of, "Well, are we published?" Clueless. She was absolutely clueless on the publishing process, even after I had explained it to her more than once.

I knew that getting something published was close to impossible. Even with all the online classes I took late at night, even with all the books and Web sites I researched on how to get published, I still wondered if it was really going to happen. I had read that it was easier to win the lottery then to get an agent, let alone have a successful book. But before children I had come from a world of statistics, and somewhere from inside of me came the old mantra of *Anything is possible—it's just a numbers game.*

So, just like in my corporate world, I didn't take the rejection letters personally. Well, maybe a little. Okay, I lied; I did take it personally—I just never let on like I did.

I felt like an island, alone in the process of getting our book out there. Blake didn't get it either. "So, Tate, when are you going to make some money on that book?" But right when I least expected it, when I felt like a complete failure and couldn't take another rejection letter, Alex came through for me with, "Don't worry Mommy, it will happen." Kids. Remarkable when you're not even looking. He gave me the strength to carry on.

I thought about submitting directly to publishers but decided not to when I read in one of my favorite sites, "One dare not go directly to a publisher without an agent. It is like going shopping without your clothes on; you need protection and you need to follow the endless rules ..."

But then a miracle came. Blake saw how much work I was doing and showed up. Right out of the blue when he was going to bed and I was still on my computer he did something loving and wonderful—he gave me Saturdays off. That's right, he let me have an interruption-free day. No children asking, screaming or fighting for things. Quiet, unviolated quiet so I could work on getting the book published. He finally saw that I was serious.

And then it came, right in front of me and in my grasp, an answer that I thought would never come. Being so used to rejection, I didn't even open the letter right away, giving myself time to prepare for the standard negative response. But instead of something to add to the mounting pile—of refusal, of denunciation—the glimmer of hope that I was looking for was there.

The letter basically said, "Call me." And then, when the call was made to the warm body who said, "I like your book," I was knocked out cold.

"But do you like the illustrations too?"

"Sometimes more than the words!"

He got it. He got *us*.

That's right, we found an agent, who in turn found a publisher who agreed to publish our book about a boy's blanket that teaches about giving up fear and allowing love. And then guess what? It sold. Not just fifteen thousand copies, which was the original print run, but more than we could have thought. We were in all our favorite bookstores, and even some we didn't know. We signed books and read from them to parents and to kids who laughed and squirmed and cried—not tears of joy, but tears of *I'm tired of waiting in line*. We were living our dream, outside of the good-mom dream.

It happened; we were famous to children other than our own due to one silly, hopeful book. It didn't happen right away—in fact, it took over a year—but it felt like it had when we looked back.

It was the beginning of what was to come.

But the best part, once we did get published and before things actually sold, was Blake. Blake said the words that he used to say that always made me smile. They were the words he'd say before we had kids, before we got married. He said, "You're my great independent lady."

And I felt like I was, for a moment.

CHAPTER
Thirty

"I let forgiveness rest upon all things, for thus forgiveness will be given me."

I can't remember a day that I had ten minutes to myself—what's new?

Cole is opening the bathroom door as I am changing my tampon. "What are you doing?"

"Changing ... uh ..."

"Why you doing that?" he asks. Then I'm stuck trying to answer something I'm not prepared to answer. *Why isn't that question in* Parents *magazine with a list of politically correct responses?*

Or when I am getting out of my jammies and in walks Alex as I put on my sports bra: "Why are your boobies so sad?"

"Huh?"

"They're so droopy."

I was back to the never-a-second-to-fix-breakfast-for-myself-because-I'm overwhelmed-with-the-morning-rush-and-out-the-door-on-time routine. And on the rare days that we are on time out the door, there's, "Mommy, I gotta go potty." I smelled something as I was helping them with their shoes, and sure enough, the four-year-old pooped his pants.

"Did you go poopie, Cole?"

His response, "No, Mommy, I'm a big boy now and I go in the potty, all by myself!" So I sniff his ass to check if it was just gas, and *BAM*—mud pie in the eye.

There is the unceasing, "Mommy, I want candy!" Even in the morning, when you're just trying to get them to eat something wholesome and healthy.

"What? You haven't even had breakfast." And you almost let them get away with it because they don't let up: they ask you a hundred times for it, and they pour on the whine and start throwing stuff and then throwing punches at each other even with the firm but loving, "What are the rules in our home?" That's the rhetorical question you use so you don't flat out say, "No! No! No! Stop it! What is wrong with you?! Why can't you stop it?!"

And then the mind chatter makes its way into your brain and makes your brain start to rot.

"Mommy, can I watch TV?" is the next question. This is after the toast has been bitten into the shape of a gun that is then aimed at his brother's head.

And you want so badly to let them watch just a little TV because it would be so easy to let their little minds decay while you have a precious few seconds of peace—peace and quiet. But they have already had half an hour of TV—which all experts say is the recommended daily dosage before brain gangrene—and it isn't even eight A.M. And you hate to see your children end up retarded or selling drugs because they got too much television, but you don't care because you just want to get out of the house on time. So you let them watch another half an hour so you can wash the poop off your hands or brush your teeth or start the dishwasher while they have lost all retention of their ABCs and numbers because they went from the PBS channel to the bad cartoon channel—the violent one that uses bad words and portrays women as sex kittens who look like whores.

"Come on guys, we gotta go *now*! It's *Scoobie-Doo* time." Our family code for *let's move it.*

"But I want to watch TV now!" said with that sharp and ugly whine and part-fake cry that makes you want to strangle him. *Where is his decency?*

Cole has been changed and hands washed clean. The clock says we will be late, and as I enter the parking lot while the perfect moms exit, I will get that look that says, *Those poor children. Their loser mom is always late, and she doesn't even work; she doodles or writes poetry or something. Why can't she take a shower and look more presentable?*

I'm running so fast. I'm running so fast that I forget so many things. Like my underwear is showing because Cole was pulling on my pants to get my attention, like the mascara that I put on yesterday that has become a smudge making its way down my face, resting in the bags under my eyes, making me look so old and ugly. Just a second. Just a second—I can't breathe. I can't think. What is it I was supposed to be doing?

So they are finally dropped off and it is a moment to let out a breath and look in the mirror, only to think, *Oh my God is that booger really there? Why didn't anyone say anything?*

Heading for the fueling station—Starbucks—I hit the

send button on my cell phone, thinking I shouldn't be driving and talking on the phone, and Katie picks up after the second ring. Her kids have been in school for at least an hour, so she is of course more relaxed.

"How do you know I'm doing the right thing?" I plead. She knows I'm talking about the kids, and more specifically Cole, who's in preschool now four days a week, because it still haunts me throughout the day.

"We've been through this—because it's scientific."

"Come again?"

"When you give birth to a child, that child sheds cells of itself into the mother that stay within the mother's body 'til the day she dies."

"Meaning?"

"There's a scientific reason for mother's intuition."

"And my intuition says I don't know if this is the right thing to do!"

"No, that's your head. Your intuition is the voice you hear when you're quiet that gives you that solid gut feel. So take a deep breath or two and quiet yourself, then ask."

"Uhm. I'll do that later," I say, pushing out my lower lip; my ruffled brow says, *Really, there's a scientific reason?*

"Yeah." Like, *Sure you will.*

In the parking lot, I put the car in park and admit to her, "I'm nervous."

"About?"

"I'm nervous that my life is changing and I'm not quite ready for it. I think I need to do these books because I believe that writing satiates my mind and maybe my soul and will offer me a chance to serve or something. Why is it so tough to do the things you love when you have kids?"

"Because something has to give, and that sometimes means not spending the time you want with them."

"When I'm with them all the time, I need time for me, but then when I do something for myself, I want to be with them. I'm twisted. Why can't I get it right?"

The next day I was even more warped.

It was the first time I would not be able to be there for Alex and Cole—mostly Alex. We had a book signing out of town and he had a performance at school. I was torn in half, and my heart was broken into countless pieces.

That morning after showering and blow-drying my hair, feeling like I'm not going fast enough, Cole sits at my feet with a chubby book the size of his father's palm and pleads, "Mommy, would you read to me?" My eyes glance at my watch, which shows I'm already off schedule and they will most likely be late for school. "Please, Mommy," he says so softly. I'm late, I can't, and in that moment I am anguished with guilt.

I feel the rush of what needs to be done, like bad adrenaline from crack or speed. There is no time for Cole's book. "We can read that when Mommy gets home." He pouts his lip out and says nothing and I know this is one of the many moments that I will never get back. This is that exact and precise instant where I am ripped in two.

We make it out of the house with no one crying—yet.

It's not like I'm away from the kids every day, but it is enough to make me feel crumbly and not whole.

Alex takes his backpack and heads out of the car. Cole is already at preschool and I'm minutes late for the airport. I squat next to him, pull him close so that he can feel my breath on his face and say, "You are a brave soldier and you are going to have a spectacular performance, because no matter what happens, you are fantastic!"

"Mommy, don't go."

"I will be there; not in body but in spirit."

Tears run down his face. "I want your body."

"I know. But my spirit is who I really am—it will be wrapped around tightly hugging you, embracing you. My words will be in your head telling you how much I love you."

And there it was—the big ugly cry, lower lip quivering, tears gushing, nose dripping, and face red.

I pull him in close and swallow him up in my arms. I kiss his neck and the back of his head. Then slowly, very slowly, I pull us apart and look at his tiny hand, look at his finger-nails that are the same as my husband's and whisper as I put his small hand over my heart, "Do you feel that?"

"Nu-uh."

"Close your eyes and see if you feel my heartbeat."

"Maybe a little," he lies nicely.

Then I take his hand and I put it over his heart.

"Do you feel that?"

"No."

"Well, if you get real quiet, you will feel my heartbeat over your heart, and it will stay there. If you get sad or scared, remember my heartbeat is hugging your heart."

My hand is still on his chest.

"I will be there every minute that you are there; I will not miss one beat, because my love will be all around you."

"Mommy, I want all of you, not parts."

So I kiss his hand and leave a lipstick imprint and say, "Every time you feel like I am not there, look at your hand and it will be proof that I am there."

"Well, what happens if the kiss mark goes away?"

"Then I'll be the invisible power that walks in front of you and behind you."

He still isn't buying it, but at least his crying stopped; he takes his backpack, leaves the curb and walks toward his class. I want to carry him in there but know that would be over-the-top, too clingy, too much. But I want to do it anyway.

I watch his small body and see the movements of a random sniffle here and there, his shoulders slumped, his sadness still heavy.

I get in my car, brush a hair out of my face, and head to the airport. It was when I was on the plane that I noticed that the smell of my children stayed on my hands even hours after I had left them.

CHAPTER
Thirty-One

"This instant is the only time there is."

Christmas.
    Something had gotten into Blake other than too much nutmeg-laced egg nog. He wanted to go east for the holidays. He wanted to be in the cold. The dry cold that chaps your hands, face, and lips and leaves behind hair that needs a bottle of conditioner. The cold that makes things brittle to the point where more than a tree branch wants to snap.

He was wearing a white turtleneck and a navy blue v-neck pullover, which made his chin look strong. Blake doesn't go to the gym these days and he hasn't been running, and I've noticed he's been dressing to look trimmer. Hiding what lies beneath. I'd like to put him on the flat-belly meal plan, but that would never work—maybe I should try it for myself. It's not only girls who wear layers to hide the things that we don't want everyone to see. My husband is proof. However, given my body's shape, I don't think it's in the cards for me to ever say, "Hey muscle man, would you give me a good flex."

His parents were going to be in Florida for Christmas; they said they needed a good thaw and wanted to spend more time with the other grandkids—Blake's sister's family. So we had their house, and Blake wanted to make it the best Christmas ever, as if he were replacing his past with the present, creating something good from what once was bad.

His parents live in rural Pennsylvania. Their house is just like all the others on the street: small, plain, with unkempt lawns. Heavy maples and red, mature oaks are scattered across the bare landscape. There's a stone wall on the right side as we approach the house. It was once a wall to the pasture owned by a farmer—his dad told me it was over a hundred and fifty years old. A perfect, quaint house to have grown up in ... or was it?

There would be few Christmas decorations. His parents didn't bother anymore; the only effort made was the ornamental tree that lived in the basement, and Blake wasn't going near that, not even with a gun to his head. We were going to cut down a tree at a Christmas tree farm fifteen minutes away and live a Norman Rockwell picture, or at least that was the plan.

Knowing there would be sparse Christmas paraphernalia, Blake, being on an all-time Christmas high, decided to order a few things before our arrival. "Honey, I got this great Christmas stuff from a catalog. It's going to make my parents' house look really awesome." I nodded and smiled at him, like, *Good idea*, but inside I had my doubts. He wasn't a catalog shopper.

He had planned this trip for months, rearranged his schedule—we would be there for two and a half weeks. It was hard to tell who was more excited on the way to the airport, Blake or the kids. They shared their visions of their winterland dream. That all came to a crashing halt when we were reminded that we live on the planet earth and not the planet of fantasies.

Having arrived at the airport one and a half hours before takeoff, we were stuck in a long line, a hundred people deep. We finally did get to the ticket counter, only to find out that the plane was oversold and "Your family won't be able to sit together. And there will be a short delay."

We boarded fifty-six long minutes after departure time and sat three hours on the tarmac before takeoff. It was only fitting we would miss our connecting flight. Short on nutritious food and fresh air, we found ourselves stranded in O'Hare Airport with no luggage and no flights until the next morning.

No problem. The airline put us up in a room at a "new" Ramada. New, if new means younger than twenty years— twenty years of no maintenance.

The kids were thrilled to jump on a hotel bed like a trampoline and have room service— which didn't exist at midnight. Blake wasn't so easily amused. But the next day we got a second wind after four and a half hours of sleep and hopes of soon being at our holiday destination. The good news was that we did see snow on his parents' front lawn—three delays and twelve hours later.

It wasn't the sleep deprivation or the fact that both kids got the stomach flu on the day that we arrived (only to find out that the washer was broken) that got Blake down. It wasn't even the rain that melted the snow and made everything grey and ugly that made him sad. Nor was it the mounting puke-ridden sheets and towels from the kids' vomit that couldn't be washed right away because only one repairman worked that close to Christmas in the small town where we were. It wasn't the absence of our Christmas packages that I had forwarded to the house—the kids' presents from Santa—that got him blue. It was that the stuff he'd ordered to fill the house and trim the tree with yuletide spirit hadn't come yet.

But then the day when God was kind and let a miracle happen—his package arrived. The kids were now feeling better, the sheets were clean, the washer was working. We were feeling like ourselves again.

The day before Christmas, I realize there's nothing in the fridge and it's close to dinnertime. The kids would be hungry soon. So I give Blake a break and declare, "Blake, I'm taking the boys to the grocery store. Why don't you take a breather." I hope he'll take advantage of a moment alone in his old home to either unwind or gear up for the big holiday right around the corner.

When we arrive back to the house with groceries and dinner, it's dark outside. It has been a while since our last trip to Blake's parents' house, and the darkness from short winter days makes it hard to find the house. It's not that I had lost my way or forgotten which turn to make or even which street they lived on. Their house was hard to recognize because it had turned into a different house. It wasn't a house like all the others with white lights dripping from the eaves like sparkling icicles. Nor was it a house with an elegant wreath and light from a single candle in each window. It was something else. Something had gone terribly, horrifyingly wrong.

It was *Christmas Vacation* on steroids all in one light fixture—an enormous green neon wreath with a red neon bow that shined brighter than a trillion-watt bulb. It was blinding, deafening, mind-altering. The boys in the back screamed, "Wow! Wow, Mommy, we have the brightest house in the neighborhood!" The brightest house in this galaxy was more like it.

I stumble into the house like a deer caught in headlights—very high beams. I feel the walls for stability. I stumble and then crash to the floor, pretending to be blind and dying.

"What?" Blake says, like, *Come on.*

I'm on my knees crawling and feeling around like a blind man, then I find a child and attach my fingers to his face. "Cole, Cole, is that you?"

"Yes, Mommy."

"Oh, thank God!" I say, hugging him desperately.

"Come on, Tate, what's wrong?"

"Nothing, honey. It's just a little bright out there, that's all."

"I'm not done!" he says emphatically.

"Thank God." I find Blake's eyes and smile softly. "They actually have industrial dimmers?"

He walks away; he isn't easily amused. Then he walks back toward me.

"You know, when I was putting it up, the Johnsons from across the street loved it; they even applauded."

"Yeah, they were clapping." I'm imitating someone clapping in slow motion, with a trancelike smile planted on my face like a bad actor. "And they were thinking, *Poor Blakie. Look at what happens when you move to California; you turn into one of those Lala-landers who think Vegas lights are a good thing.*"

Before therapy, he would have been so pissed, missing the joke or taking it the wrong way and storming off. But we have been in therapy for a while now and we can find humor again. He comes over and gives me a noogie on my head.

I thought it was the disastrous, high-voltage, neon fixture that had Blake all bummed out. Not a chance. It was something deeper and more painful. A ghost of memories in his old home. The pain came back.

His alcoholic father, raging and ranting the night before Christmas, came in through his memory bank, and the doom and the gloom before the dawn of each morning jolted his system. Blake wouldn't talk much—he couldn't even if he tried. Tongue-tied heart.

But he didn't have a chance to sulk in his own murkiness; it was Christmas Eve, and the kids would be coming down the steps not many hours later. I hung the stockings after filling them with candy, which I bought after they were in bed. There was last-minute wrapping and placing of the gifts and getting the house ready for Santa.

He was sipping a cocktail—a rarity. I didn't press, I didn't pry. I just kept busy until he finally spoke his first word close to midnight. "I'm sorry I brought us here."

"What? Why?"

"I thought it would be better, I thought I could make it right—what a bust."

I walk over, scissors and tape in one hand, damp dishrag in the other, and bend down next to him like I do for my children and say, "Hey, Christmas hasn't even started—our vacation has just begun."

He doesn't say anything. His failure too big to be changed in his head, he concedes, "I think I lost what I think I had—I think I've lost my way home."

Wow! I'm thinking, *Blake has never said anything so honest and so real about himself ever—so open and valid.* I touch his knee lightly as I note, "You haven't lost your way; it's always been with you, right inside your heart."

He can't say anything because he wants to believe what

I have just said but he's not there, not capable of really getting it—yet. I try to come up with something encouraging, something that will pull him out of his feelings of heaviness, something that will draw him out of the bad memories that run through his mind in this house. I try to find something in my brain that would make me feel better; all I can come up with is, "The problem with you is that you don't ask for too much; you ask for too little. If God could ask you anything he would say, *Is that all you wanted?*"

Somehow it hits a chord and he smiles at me thankfully. "So what's next—what else needs to be wrapped?" He takes the dish towel from my hand and asks, "Who gets this?"

When we did make it to bed, the bed was dressed with a sleek blanket—sensual and glossy. It was perfect for wrapping us together. I take off my clothes; he is already in bed when he says, "Bring that beautiful body over here and shake your hair in my face." I laugh and walk over to oblige.

Thirty-Two

"I rule my mind, which I alone must rule."

At home, I pick up the phone. There is a drizzle of rain, the sky is grey and the mood is somber. I have already lit the candles on my altar and given thanks. I feel uncertain of the day and where it will lead. The house is quiet. I have dropped Blake at the airport for a business trip, right after I had taken Cole to kindergarten.

As I clean up the last bits of Cole's breakfast, I think about Katie. We never talk about Jack, I mean really talk about what's going on with him—or with them. I had been so busy trying to maintain my sanity while also working on the book and taking care of the kids that I'd stopped pushing her to talk about it—and she would never have brought it up herself. It's almost as if his cancer never existed.

After punching in the tenth number and after the second ring, Katie's voice is relaxed on the other end. As soon as she recognizes my voice she says, "Do you have any idea how grateful I am that I have you as a best friend?"

"Yep," I say.

"No, really, I'm serious."

"I am too." And I mean it.

"It's calm when I'm with you, my head stops spinning, I don't feel like everything that I do is a complete failure—"

"Wow, that doesn't sound like you at all." *Good. Maybe today I can get her to talk.*

"No. I'm serious." She then adds, "I'm healed when I am around you, more myself. The good parts shine through. It's as if we increase the vibrancy of one another, enhance each other—like the rough edges get smoother. Maybe that's it— our rough edges meet the other's rough edges to makes us smooth, like a tumbled stone. I forget my way to myself so much more now that I am this person."

"What person?" She makes no comment. The feelings of uncertainty float around me. I want to know the details of what's going on in her life; her kids, how *is* she, has she started therapy yet. It's bubbling under the surface—leaving a dead space of silence.

"What are you doing?" she asks.

"It's quiet."

"Oh yeah. How did it go with the numbers?" She's talking book sales.

"Life is going to bite you in the ass a million times; it's all about the padded underwear!"

"Was it that bad?"

"Nah, it was fine—there are a few articles about the book that are getting some play, but sales are slowing down."

"Fleeting," she says.

"Maybe not."

"How do you get free when you feel so dug in?" Now we're going somewhere.

"Dig out."

"Right, it's that easy."

"It can be."

"When did our roles reverse?"

"When Jack went for chemo."

Silence.

"How's Blake?"

"I gotta say, he is really trying. He's better with me and the kids. Picking up around the house, taking them to school, putting them to bed—giving me more time to take a breath. I have no complaints."

And it's true. It's as if someone has taken a big eraser and softened the edges of my life with Blake—at least for the moment. I hope the things that bugged me before therapy have stopped.

I have begun to sit with the boys at breakfast and eat with them. We play games, slowing down our breath when they get worked up, and if that doesn't work they go to a place to self-quiet. It works sometimes, and the other times they go back to ignoring me.

But the best change has been me—I'm growing up. I hear my therapist in my head as I walk through my life. And I started to realize that Blake wasn't taking my power away, I was giving it to him. Once I was reminded that I could claim it back, my life began to magically work. I stopped holding on to my life so tightly, suffocating and smothering my wants, and I began to look for moments of contentment.

"Huh?" she says. "When did you find happiness?"

"I think it's always been there, it was just covered up by my anger. When I get moments right, I try to hold on to them. I've taken your advice on meditating more, and reading. And doing the work from therapy."

She interrupts my preaching on self-help to talk about nothing, nothing I want her to talk about. I hope she'll go to the root of her feelings about Jack. Maybe, finally, she will be smart enough to go to the core of it. But she says nothing, so I get to it by using myself as an example.

"When my dad came out to visit at Thanksgiving, he was really trying to be nice and on his best behavior, really trying to be accommodating and helpful, but his anger was there to pop out anytime. So he tried to hide it and hold it down and it became this built-up pressure. But you could tell he was really, really trying to be kind. He let me get out of the house, out of the way of him and out of the way of myself trying to hold it all together but not really holding it together. It was like he could lose it right under my nose, inches away from me—a screaming match that didn't happen but could." In my mind's eye, I see him standing in my kitchen, tall and dark, his hair almost all white, making himself a cup of coffee. Still mad at the world, the same anger that carried him through his life; my siblings and I were enveloped in it alongside him.

Soon the throttle of rage that he taught me would be at my fingertips, and I could turn into a screamer and a punisher to my kids, who were sitting at the table being perfectly normal kids. When I was barely older than Alex, I would have liked a hit man to remove my dad from the street I grew up on. I didn't want Alex to feel that way about me.

She caught me in my daydream. "Ah-ha! The truth will set you free."

"Huh?"

"You are experiencing the human condition. Why do you always think that there is something dreadfully wrong with you when you are so damn normal?"

"That's not it."

"Hey, reality check, people don't talk about their neuroses—they hide them, or don't deal with them, or push them down, suppress. You feel your feelings and are with them intimately—go ahead, give them a cup of tea, welcome them and then let them go when they are ready."

"Like with Jack"

"What?" She sounds hurt.

"Well, how is it going?"

"Fine," she says defiantly.

"Why can't the tables turn? Why can't you open up?"

"Because there's nothing to say," she says calmly, in denial.

"Really?"

"Yes," she says again in a matter-of-fact way.

"Shut up." I mean it.

She continues to preach, "You need to clear your head. This isn't about me. It's about you." And she means it.

"What?"

"I'M SERIOUS," she says forcefully.

"Geez, I'm okay with my dad, I'm okay with my life."

"Take a deep breath," Katie says quietly.

Now *I'm* pissed as I fume, "Like a deep fucking breath? Would that be through my mouth, nose, or vagina?" I'm frustrated. Why does she have to be the therapist all the time?

"Tate!"

"Okay, okay ... just a minute." I need a minute to get my mind around this. I need to defuse this craziness. So I take the phone into the study where the small tea-light candles are still flickering, and their light dances to a breeze that cannot be seen. I sit on the sofa and let my eyes soften on the glow of the candlelight. I breathe deeply through my nostrils and let my shoulders relax. I let the second breath out even slower. I take another and my body begins to relax and I ask God not to heal me but to heal her. I hear her voice coaching me through the speakerphone, "Picture a white golden light in the center of your mind and release all thoughts. Let your body bend and sway as if it were on a hammock, and just breathe."

I feel her voice become calmer and slower as I let her hypnotize herself along with me. My eyes are closed and I have let myself slow down; I listen for my heartbeat that quiets my thoughts, and then my eyes pop open. She is crying; she finally has started to cry.

"What's wrong?" I ask gently.

"Okay. I think he's not okay and I don't have the strength to deal with it."

I want to say *Hallelujah*, but instead say, "That's okay," trying to give her the space to talk.

She doesn't respond. But then after a long pause, she asks, "Can we drop this?"

"When I am writing or working on the books, I feel whole, complete, and I feel on purpose, like I am doing something for myself, like I'm doing what I was meant to be doing, outside of my children. And when I write, even if I don't make it to the gym, or get a shower, I still have a good day. I feel like the kids are behaving better, and I can handle whatever they're up to."

"I get it," Katie says matter-of-factly.

"No, I'm serious."

"So am I. I get it. I feel the same when I paint, draw, or doodle, or do something creative for myself, even if I'm zapped ...'Do the thing you love, and the rest will follow'... I guess the expression should be 'Do the thing you love every day and you will be sane.'"

"You do get it—okay, now let's get real." I take a slow breath but make sure she doesn't hear it. "How's it going? Come on, how's it really going?"

She pauses before answering, "I don't know." "Sometimes working on our art isn't enough. It can't fully heal us; sometimes we need help," I offer.

"I know, I know. We've been talking about going to a therapist."

"Okay." *Wow, I can't believe she just said that and I can't believe how calm I am right now and please, please keep talking Katie.*

"He's different," she says, her voice cracking.

"Yeah."

"He's more vulnerable and needy. I don't have the strength. The strange thing is, he's now open to looking at his life differently—he's now open to searching."

"What's he searching for?"

"Who knows?" She sounds tired when she says this.

"Yeah, and … ?"

"And nothing—that's it," she lets out a sigh.

"Okay."

"Yeah, yeah, yeah."

I know her face on the other side of the phone, it's her intense face that you rarely see because she doesn't have an answer, because she is struggling but trying to be stoic. This is where I stay quiet and hold the space in my consciousness, because if I just stay really still, she will say something.

This is a big move for Katie—the master of suppression. She can't help being this way—it's the way she was trained by her mother, who was trained by her grandmother; the recipe for living, handed down from generation to generation. The not-feeling recipe. The denial recipe. She is on the cusp of finding the error of tradition, a crack in the blue-blood sidewalk.

"I wish I could help him." Her voice is intense, it almost sounds like it will splinter.

"I know, angel—"

Now she does cry the ugly cry. "He really has to do this thing—this stuff—this search of himself on his own, and it's so frustrating because I want to help, but I can't."

"I know, baby. God, can I come up to see you?"

"No, no, it's okay. I'm okay. It's just that he's moving at such a snail's pace."

"It's not a race."

"I know, I know. I get it. I get it."

She won't talk much more, she won't expand on how the kids are dealing with and facing it all; she won't because she can't and I understand. I understand her; she will when she will. So, I let her get off the phone first as I slowly put the handset in the cradle and I let out a meek prayer of love and peace for her, and I hope that my heart is strong and powerful enough to let my prayer sail like the wind to her heart and comfort her.

CHAPTER
Thirty-Three

"It can be but myself I crucify."

In the grind of the day-to-day routines, I thought my marriage was back on track. I thought things were back to perfect. Hardly. How can you be so happy one minute and so miserable and disconnected the next? Our marriage was bipolar.

Life felt hard and full of twists and turns with gnarled roads that grabbed at my ankles. Just when I thought I was running, skipping through my life, right when I thought I had it right and was floating in my heavenly thoughts, I got slapped back to earth into my three-dimensional being.

I wasn't alone in my thinking. Blake and I figured we could skip a few sessions in therapy and our marriage would magically transform into a perpetually blissful state—wrong. We used the excuse that it was a waste of money and convinced ourselves that our therapist wasn't really that good—which of course was a lie.

Transformation isn't automatic—it's a process of shoveling through your pain, looking at it, dealing with it and taking two steps forward. Then, when you've forgotten how it got there, take one step back. When we stopped going to therapy, we stopped working on our marriage and supporting one another, and things turned to crap. We were steps backward, back to the blaming game sprinkled with no sex. Our frustration brought us back to our next session. I couldn't believe that weeks ago I loved my husband and now I wanted to kill him. No, I mean it—I really wanted to kill him.

"It's been a while," is the first thing our therapist says after she sees we are settled into our chairs.

"Yeah," we confess and succumb to our error.

"So tell me, what's going on?"

I want to say, *I'm back to hating him, right when I thought I loved him again. What's up with that, doc?* But instead I say, "I think we're in a rut."

"Okay," she says, prodding us on. Blake says nothing; stiff as a board—typical.

"It's been so busy with the kids that we have stopped going out on date nights." I don't know why I just confessed that, it is no surprise what she is going to say.

"So, how is that working for you?" she asks in a kidding tone.

"Well, not so good."

"Blake, so how's it going for you?" she asks, like she doesn't believe what I just said and needs a second opinion. He shrugs his shoulders like, *I don't think anything is wrong, it's all her stuff.*

There are so many things that I hate about my husband in that moment that I don't know where to begin. So I start with the catalyst that made me call for the appointment. "I want to talk about what happened on Saturday."

Blake turns red and is clearly uncomfortable. But I don't care; he started this mess. I try not to be angry, but it comes out in my tone. "You know, for most families Saturday is a family day, to go bike riding, or out to a museum. Not a chance with us. *Blake* decides to go through closets and the whole house and *organize*. But this is how he does it. First, he takes all his personal stuff—his belongings, the things he owns—and affectionately organizes what he wants to save, puts it gently in a shoe box, stores it in a safe and tidy place or moves it to another part of the house or maybe gives it to the Salvation Army. His stuff is tenderly cared for."

I am looking straight at my therapist as I continue. "Everyone else's stuff is thrown in a heap. If there are breakables, tough luck, they'll be broken—like picture frames or delicate and fragile things—the things that you love will be destroyed." Blake is not amused as I continue. "But he doesn't care. He's on his mission. It's like he's saying, 'This is what I think of you. I'll throw you in a heap, where you belong.'" I say this with a tossing hand motion.

Blake interrupts in a pathetic voice, "That's not true."

I ignore his remark. "Oh, that's not the best part. When he's going through this area, a walk-in closet for example, you'll know what he's doing because he announces it with his grunts and cruel remarks, like, 'What the hell is this and why is it here?' So I ask to help or offer to work with him, but I might as well be asking, 'Could you please put boric acid in my eyes?' or 'I would love for you to cut my head off with a rusty saw.' Because that's what you are going to get, not a man who is grumpy, not a man who's slightly irritated, but a man who is ruthless and mean." I don't mention that he makes faces when he does this, like, *Please feel sorry for me as I go through your shit. And it doesn't matter that you didn't ask—this needs to be done, and I am doing it now!*"

My therapist stops me. "Blake, I know you are uncomfortable. You will have a chance to explain your side of the story, just try to breathe." She says this so lovingly that I think the two of them should go off and get a room. But I am on a roll, and this has been bugging me, so I continue. "Then, when the dust settles and he's 'finished' cleaning the space, he'll leave a note, 'Could you go through this?' It might as well say, 'Could you go through your shit now, and then roll over and die?'"

In my mind I see it happening, and my heart is crushed by the memory. And when it was all over I went to the pile of things and saw the treasures that were dear to me broken. My heart, which had been broken before by this man, began to rip deeper in the center, leaving a hole that made me feel so lost. And then the hurt of my broken heart leaks out a burning heat that makes its way up my throat as tears roll down my face to cool off the pain.

I am surprised how quickly the tears come as I talk through them. "He's made a mess of something that wasn't a mess before. He has contaminated it; he ruined my special picture frame and tore a favorite piece of clothing that I was saving for a rainy day. And I hate him for it. I want to divorce him and I wish that I never met him."

That's when she stops me, really stops me, interceding with, "Blake, would you mind grabbing a magazine? I want to talk to Tate for a second. I'll get you when we can talk about this together."

When she closes the door, I don't let her coach me; instead I pour out, "I thought he would change his ways. He's done this before. He tells me he is sorry in therapy, and I forgive him, but six months later he does it again. And this time he has cut out a little piece of my heart, this time he has taken a little bit of my soul, and this time I'm too hurt to forgive him, because last time when I forgave him I believed he would change—and he didn't. This time the wall is around my heart to keep him out."

"And you feel like you will be safe if you don't let him in?" she offers.

"Yeah," I say, looking at the floor.

"So, what did you do?"

The heaviness on my chest is too much—a sinking feeling making me feel so lost, so sad. Like if it doesn't stop I'm going to start to cry again and that won't be enough. It won't be enough to release the pain. It's too heavy, it's too heavy. Stop. It's too late, I'm crying, choking in fact. It's over, I've crumbled. "He's got blind spots and I don't mean visual, I mean mental. He is so focused on the stuff that doesn't matter and he loses track of what's going on inside—aging radar, heading towards crashville." She lets me continue to purge, her face is so kind when I say, "He makes me nuts when he's eating, always making noises while chewing. Sucking on his fingers—yuck. I can't help but listen, it's too loud. He's too loud, too heavy. I feel suffocated by his weight. And another thing, I'm sick of having everything on a dimmer; I feel like I'm in a deep dark hole unable to see what is in front of me: a bad marriage trying to survive. 'Everything's got a soft romantic glow,' he says. 'That's what dimmers do.' But it's not romantic, it's dark. Why can't he see that it's too dark and that you can't see anything? Okay, sometimes it enhances the mood when I'm pissed off, when I can't see the food I'm eating, like I'm trying to erase what is really happening to me."

She finally stops my endless ramble. "Tate, how are you taking care of yourself? Have you been doing the things you love—writing and meditating?"

"Well, no."

"Our words are powerful. You create what you state. If

you keep telling him you hate him and want to divorce him, that's where you will go. I see it all the time. Do you want to get a divorce?"

I shake my head no.

"When you tell him he's a bad person, or a bad husband, do you see how it affects him? How would you feel if he said those things to you? It would kill you," she says, nodding toward me.

I don't like what she is saying, but I believe her. She launches into a speech about taking care of myself, not taking Blake's actions personally, going back to the data log of when he does support me, changing my communication. It's all about the *schema*—changing our core belief that we lack the other's support.

She catches me rolling my eyes. "You have to spell it out for men. You have to let him know what you are doing so he can acknowledge you. For example, 'Just to let you know, I picked up your laundry at the cleaners and it's in the closet.' Give him the opportunity to say *thank you* for something you did, and *receive* the compliment. Notice the shift in support."

I can see she knows I'm not buying it. She can't read my thoughts—*Just more work. I want him to change without having to help him*—but she gets the drift.

So she adds, "I think I want to do individual sessions with each of you and then have one together. In the meantime, keep on working on the things you love—the books, meditation—and when you want to blame him, or tell him all the things that you don't like, stop. Wait, reflect, and go back and try to connect to him. Look in his eyes and find the love, because it's there. He loves you, Tate, and he's a good guy. Remember, you have to spell it out for men. Tell him what you want in a positive way—'It makes me happy when you.' We can cover more next time."

Then Blake comes in and she talks to him alone, and then we leave. But unlike most times, I don't feel better; I feel as if I have lost.

When I am home, I want to talk to someone, but Katie isn't the right person. Then I pick up the phone to call Ann—my new friend. My friend who likes and respects me. She likes my new perspective of transformational living, and luckily she doesn't know all my history or all the baggage and all the pain and neurosis.

Maybe I can have idle chit-chat with her and feel loved.

That's what it's like when you find a new girlfriend; it's like playdates that are pure fun. You get that endorphin rush of camaraderie—someone who cares. It's early in our friendship, she thinks I am cool, and I feel the same way about her.

Pretty soon we'll be family-dating to see if our husbands like each other as much as we do, and then the kids. It's hard to family date. Just when you get it right with the moms, the dads screw it up with their incompatibilities. And then you have to go through the divorce and the search for a new family that fits—they're few and hard to find.

What I know about her husband is good, and the kids have already played and had fun—the dating may be a success. She has come over to our house and we have gone to theirs. We feel comfortable with each other. We laugh a lot, and it's so nice how our friendship has moved forward.

If I'm not careful I could easily stalk her—calling her every day to see what she's doing. But we aren't there yet; we're still putting in a foundation.

I hit the talk button and punch in her number, which I know by heart. Answering machine, so I leave a message. It's just as well—I don't want to scare her away.

CHAPTER Thirty-Four

"I am not a body. I am free."

I take the soft, white tissue and blow my nose, and out comes green sludge; not yellow, but green, dark green. Now I know I'm really sick. Before this I was in denial, thinking it would go away; now I have no choice, because it is here and it is here to stay if I don't take immediate action. My nose is chapped and sore. I smear Tiger Balm under it, which leaves behind a slippery red surface. Now it looks like I have a permanent layer of snot on my upper lip.

I cough, and now I spit out mucus that is woody-green, clumped in nuggets of infection. I head for the cabinet for the Chinese herbs; it's Saturday, and no doctor will see me 'til Monday. I feel like crap; my body aches, my thoughts and movements are slow, and that ammonia-like taste of phlegm that sticks in the back of my throat won't go away—yuck.

I fill a water glass with 1000mg of vitamin C, echinacea, bee pollen, ginger, garlic, goldenseal, osha root and a Chinese mushroom combination. Cold water is run over the concoction before I gulp the whole thing down; it is bitter and fierce. I hope the slug-like bile that rests in my lungs will clear. Katie's Chinese voodoo doctor is always right, or so says Katie. She says this mixture, this potion, is better than even the best antibiotic. We shall see. She also says that our body's natural state is well-being, so I should think myself well. But my mind isn't strong enough to do that.

In the meantime, I have begged my husband to take the boys so that I can rest. He is reluctant—he wanted to go for a run, he wanted to go to Home Depot, he wanted to do all the things he loves to do for himself, with himself, by himself. He has taken Saturday's back.

The kids are safely in his car when I rub my encrusted right eye—granules of mucus turned hard. I think I have pink eye.

"How could you have let yourself get so sick?" he bitterly asks, like I have committed the ultimate crime. "You'd better be better by Monday; there's no way I can clear my schedule. You're on your own Monday. Did you hear me?" Like this should be some type of surprise to me, as if he never says this. He always says it, he never comes home early when I am sick—yeah, yeah, yeah, it's my problem, not his.

I look away and head to the closet, where I put on my red down slippers over my socks. He hates the red down booties because they shed feathers, which create "a big mess" that he has to clean up because of his compulsive-clean-freak disorder. The feathers wind him up, they aggravate him, and they irritate him like he's covered in lice.

Therefore I not only wear them, I slide and scuff *hard* on the floor to force the feathers out like sandpaper to wood, as if my feet are saying *fuck you, fuck you, fuck you, I hate you.* I rub that damn floor 'til I'm exhausted and plop in my bed, but I am too restless to lie still. I'm too mad to sleep, I hate him too much.

The phone rings. And with a thick, sick voice that sounds like a two-year-old's I say, "Hewohw." Just like Elmer Fudd.

"Hi. How are you?"

"Hey, Ann."

"You sound awful. I just made chicken soup; I'll bring some over," she says in a matter-of-fact and upbeat tone.

"What? No—" like, *That is too nice of you.*

"It's my grandmother's recipe. Sure to cure."

"Wow. Thank you so much. But you really don't have to . . .."

"Hey, Tate, when you're feeling better, would you be interested in doing a parenting class with me? My kids are driving me nuts."

"Yeah, definitely."

"Good. I'll bring the info with the soup. I'll be there in an hour." We continue to talk and I feel better, and then I hear the garage door opening.

Blake comes home before I am ready for him to come home. I haven't taken that nap yet, haven't had time for a hot bath, and I haven't read a page in the stack of books beside my bed. I didn't have time for me yet. The kids run toward me.

He comes up to ask how I am. I turn my head and I give him the cheek, like I'm giving him the middle finger. He tries to give my cheek a kiss. During the car ride home, he must have felt guilty about how mean he was and is now looking for forgiveness. Notta chance. Self-protection. Asking how I'm feeling is his way of saying sorry, but the actual words haven't left his lips.

If I return his kiss anytime, sick or not sick, or acknowledge him in any positive way, it could lead to sex, and there is no way I wanna do that; I barely have enough energy to hold my head up. I want sleep. Sex just means more exhaustion tomorrow. Not that he's asking for sex—he doesn't want to be sick. But every day he comes home from work with that kiss, that same kiss that says, *Maybe today I'll get lucky*—forget it.

Herein lies the tragedy. I hurt his feelings, he withdraws. Avoiding this problem pulls us apart, which creates another problem. This leads to more therapy, and then it's the therapist who puts in the boundary. "Kiss her with the intention that that is enough. Don't look for more, let her come to you." Our therapist puts in the boundary, which puts back the space that can create the closeness—go figure. And when I get the space I need, he then makes a touchdown on the weekend.

This sounds as if it were all resolved, right? Wrong. Well, not really wrong; it just took a long time to get to the weekend nookie. Here, let me explain: So often we have the right impulse, just the wrong solution. I set a boundary, but it's inappropriate. I build a wall and cut him off, I alienate him. It's only when the therapist suggests I try to give him a chance, to let him into my heart, that I consider lowering the wall. I try to look at him differently when he walks in the door. I focus on his eyes and the wrinkles around them and see that they are soft and kind. Or I take notice that his hair is greying and thinning—maybe I had something to do with that.

Okay, I can open my heart to him—a little. I can let out a little love in his direction and it's satisfying. It wasn't so hard. I'm okay. I try being affectionate without being tired, guilty, and overwhelmed. I try, but I don't keep it up.

Here's the problem: Reprogramming my mind and changing the way I do things takes time. It takes time to let him in when he seems so selfish, and so *male*. It takes time to identify what the real conflict is—it's not him, it starts with me. Once I figured out that all I have to do is speak to him nicely when I ask for the things I want, something shifted. I felt entitled to have him love *me* unconditionally when I was in a crisis mode, stressed and mean. But the truth is, it's hard to love someone when they are mean.

I tend to see what I was supposed to when it's too late. Like waiting until my marriage was on a frayed shoestring to figure out we are both right and both wrong. The only way I knew to express myself was to blame him for everything. The rancor just came out; I don't know where it came from, like, "I'd like to be closer if you weren't so damn needy all the time!" That never worked. Never made a point with that one. Never made him happy to hear it.

It was hard for me to figure out his motivations behind his tendencies. It was hard to respect him when he overstepped a boundary. But a good therapist can do amazing things. She showed me that we all need love, approval and understanding.

She could interpret my anger and frustration and coach me into a place of forgiveness—forgiveness of him and forgiveness of me. It was in that place that I found I could understand his feelings seriously, not mockingly and not judgingly, but really lovingly. It took a long time, but it worked and was worth the money, because what I got back was this man, who learned to love me with my flaws and see me clearly. And I was able to see how magnificent he really is.

Instead of patchworking our differences and our struggles, we found a whole intimacy that we thought stopped existing. It came down to premeditated thought. What appeared to be out of the blue was actually thought about all day. I was reading in bed and he came in and said, "You look tired. Want a foot rub?" How can you say no?

CHAPTER Thirty-Five

"No one can fail who seeks to reach the truth."

T*each your child to trust their intuition* was a lesson in the parenting class that Ann and I took together.

This was the lesson I held on to for dear life and put in our next children's book. *When the child asks what to do, instead of telling him, ask him to close his eyes, take a breath, and feel for the answers inside himself. Children look to their parents for solutions; help them to find their own.* My children began to slow down a bit before they made a decision, like what they wanted to eat and whether they could get it on their own. Somehow along the way they began to find the right answers for themselves.

Ann's timing was perfect; it's like she was psychic. I'd been wanting to explore using the good advice that I got for my marriage with my kids. Even though my children were so very different from each other, at the core they were the same, just like Blake and I.

It reminded me of when my father dropped off my big brother at college. The last thing he said before leaving was, "Study hard, laugh often, and keep your honor." When he dropped me off he said, "Relax, everything will be fine." I've often wondered whether my brother and I were really different enough to merit such different words of encouragement.

Then I had kids and knew the answer.

As you step outside into our backyard, there is a small retaining wall on the right covered with creeping ficus. The small leaves make it possible to see the stones that lie beneath. Cole's fire-engine-red trike is three inches from the wall. He will go outside this morning to take in the air and play after breakfast.

The sliding doors open with a whoosh, and the sounds of the outdoors come in. Crickets, birds, living things. The outdoor air is fresh and new. Another day to do it better.

When I signed up for the parenting class, I once again thought that this would solve the problems in our family. I took the class seriously. I took it on full force, engines forward: notepads, highlighters, extra pencils for note taking—only the tape recorder and video camera stayed home.

Our textbook became my parenting script, with the aid of sticky notes that I posted throughout the house—67 at one count. I thought the book was the answer to all my prayers. Wrong.

It's the morning rush, I mean the morning *flow*. Breakfast time. Alex is fidgeting, making farting sounds and faces where only the whites of his eyes show. He's in pajamas, with bedhead and morning-kid-stink-breath. He has still not taken his first bite of cereal with bananas, but instead has pushed the banana down with his forefingers and made missile sounds. The spoon lies untouched, and his goofing around continues for another fifteen minutes. The book said to ask the child to eat only once with meaning, and to not say it again. I'm looking for the "if that doesn't help or have any effect" section. Where's Plan B?

The kitchen chair scrapes the hardwood floor as I leap towards Cole before he falls. Too late. He has slipped and I wasn't fast enough to save him. He wails, I put down the book to place him in his chair, and then continue to read as I place the cut strawberries before him. He happily eats, unlike his big goof-off brother.

I'm back in my chair, reading the book, when Alex's feet find my knee. His toes dig into my kneecap, and then he gives me a kick. I fast-forward to the "being a pain in the ass" section or the "won't eat and needs constant attention" section; there of course is none. So I resort to the conflict section. I place my hand on his shoulder, put the book in my lap, and keep it short. "Go ahead and enjoy your breakfast. I'll be in the family room right over there." He responds with a farting noise from his armpit and ignores my suggestion. I place my cold bare feet on the floor and walk three steps before I hear, "I'm not hungry. Can I play now?"

The instructor has reminded us that the average parent says *No* too many times, over a hundred and something per day if my memory serves me. So I look for alternate phrasing: *I think you know when the right time to play is.*

"Okay," he says and heads for the toys in his bedroom. I calmly walk toward his breakfast and put it in the sink; the book says breakfast is now over. I am dying because I know he will be hungry in ten seconds, I know the tantrum and the screaming and the fit that will happen from the moment he sees his bowl gone until I drop him off at school. And I know that his teachers will think that I am a horrible mother, evil and heartless, for not giving him breakfast. *How can*

*any mother let her child go to school without eating? We're
not a third-world country.*

Capable of altruism—I at least try. It's hard to be a saint
when you're born human with so many flaws that glare in
the mirror of your own futility.

It's not as bad as I thought to stay strong and follow
the instructions given by the instructor—it's a million times
worse. Now Cole is crying and sobbing his heart-breaking
sob, complete with doe eyes and raised eyebrows that say,
Why, Mommy? Why are you not feeding my brother?

We are in the car and now Alex can't believe he actually
wasn't given food at home and starts to cry, like, *This can't
be happening to me!* He looks over to Cole in his booster
seat and Cole cries back, "Momma, Alex is hungry! Please,
give him a breakfast bar." I want to so badly, I want to turn
my car around and go get him some food, but then what
will my teacher think of me at the next parenting class?
What will Ann think?

But more importantly, what is Alex's teacher going to
think? What she will say? After all, this is the teacher who
sent a note home saying, "Your child is moving around too
much, fidgeting in his seat." Blake's response was, "Yeah,
that sounds like Alex." He just blew it off, while I was prepared to take him to a neurologist.

When we got to school, I decided to suck it up and tell
the teacher what I was doing and that Alex didn't eat his
breakfast. I included a look like, *Really, he wouldn't eat,
I'm not making this up.* To my surprise, she smiled and
said, "He'll live."

Class three and Chapter 11 of our parenting class talked
about giving your children more responsibilities and empowering them with tasks that make them feel independent
and important. I was at first aghast when they suggested

what a seven-year-old is capable of doing: preparing his own lunch every morning, making family meals, washing pets, carrying in firewood, putting gas in the car, and doing the dishes. I tried it out and was astounded by what Alex was capable of; okay, so he needed a little practice and refining, but all in all not bad.

I was wondering, my personality shining through, whether I could maybe get him to take on bigger projects. Maybe bigger projects that would instill even more self-esteem! Yeah, how about if he starts fixing the plumbing and doing minor electrical work, or maybe adjusting the tile on the roof? It can't really be that dangerous, can it?

The best part of these classes was that I got to spend time with Ann, who was now becoming a close friend. We would hang out after the class for a drink or a bite to eat. The nice thing about Ann was how supportive she was of me—she didn't bring out the competitive spirit in me like Katie on the courts. She was different; she felt good in her skin and was easy with the people around her.

"Hey, what's going on with your writing?"

"Katie and I have started a second book."

"Yeah, what's it about?" she asks with open interest.

"Acknowledging kids' good behavior and empowering them."

"Sounds familiar." We both laugh.

"Steve's getting snipped this weekend." Ann is talking about her husband.

"Really? Do you think he could talk to Blake?"

"He bought every bag of frozen peas in town, not to mention a twelve-pack of beer. One of his buddies told him his balls grew to be the size of cantaloupes because he didn't take it easy. So guess what my husband's plan is?"

"What?"

"To have Vicodin and beer cocktails and watch endless football this weekend."

We both crack up.

"The good news is that I don't have to have sex for a while."

"Lucky."

"He asked me to help him shave before he has to go in."

"They don't shave it for him?"

"Go figure."

I'm glad Katie isn't here to share in the conversation. She wouldn't get not wanting to have sex; it's something she still has, I think. Let's hope it's only with her husband. Having a new friend was like having a new perspective on life; it made my evolution easier. Or maybe it was my evolution that found my new friend.

CHAPTER

Thirty-Six

"Today I will judge nothing that occurs."

Alex would have a playdate every day if I let him. And I did let him, most of the time. Kids are less work when they are playing with someone their own size. It's a win-win. Mommies are happy, kids are happy.

Until something bad happens—really bad.

Cole and I were picking Alex up from school; Alex was soliciting moms for a playdate after he handed me his back-pack. He knew if he gently pulled on their clothing to bring them close to his big brown eyes and asked directly into their faces, he'd have a chance. A much better chance than if he asked me to ask—it's hard for a mom to turn down a six-year-old who reminds her of her own son.

He soon found out that no one was available; the boys he played with had doctors appointments, soccer, karate, swimming, basketball, or something else planned. All with the exception of Zach. Zach never had playdates; as a mat-

212

ter of fact, in the one hundred days of school so far, Zach had had only one. It's not because he wasn't a kind, cool, or fun kid; it was because both his parents worked and his caretaker didn't speak English—she didn't understand the whole playdate phenomenon. She wanted Zach home safe with her—as if that would help.

So there I was, being begged by Alex and Zach to have a playdate at our house NOW! Even Cole was chiming in, "Yeah, yeah, let Zach come over." It's hard to admit, but Zach is the cutest out of the three. His blue eyes are so big that they devour his face, and he has the perfect button nose. And he's smaller than Alex even though he's a year older.

So I half mimed and half spoke in my lame Spanish to the nanny that I was going to call Zach's mother. I went to my glove compartment and took out Alex's school roster, looked up Zach's mom's number, flipped open my cell phone and called. I knew she would be able to speak Spanish to Rosa and make the event happen or not.

"Hey, Pam, this is Alex's mom, Tate. Sorry to call last minute, and if it doesn't work we can do this another day— easily. But our kids were wondering whether Zach could come to our house and play." She already knew where we lived; we had all been to a dozen birthday parties and school performances, so we had a basic bio on each other. Still, she was definitely caught off guard. "Uh yeah, uh well, yeah. I could have Rosa pick him up after Brian's golf lesson." Brian is Zach's older brother.

"It's no problem bringing him to your home if that works better," I offer, trying to accommodate.

"Well, that might—is Rosa there?"

"Here, let me put her on." Rosa has been waiting patiently. The kids are jumping up and down; they think this playdate is going to happen.

Rosa speaks lightning-speed Spanish, and after a *Sí, Sí* she nods and hands the phone back to me.

"Tate, are you sure this is no problem?"

"No, not at all—it'll be fun."

"Would you mind dropping him off?"

"No problem."

"Okay."

She gives me directions and then I load the boys into the car. On the way to our house, the boys are giggling and cracking each other up with their butt and poopie jokes. Once inside our home, hands are washed and snacks are prepared. Zach eats anything I give him, even the healthy flax seed granola bars that my kids never eat. We play in the backyard, and then they head to the garage for more toys.

In the garage, as I'm squatting to put Cole's helmet on, Zach says close to my face, "Daddy uses the black club."

"Huh?" I say, trying to get the chin strap smaller so it fits, as Cole fidgets to set himself free.

"The black club. Daddy uses the black club."

I'm half listening. "For what?"

"When we're bad," he says, looking straight at me.

My heart sinks. "I'm sorry, Zach, could you say that again?"

I'm now looking right at him. His eyes are glued to mine like tractor beams. He is about to unload, or more likely explode, because he has been wanting to say this for some time, and then he pours out, "Daddy uses the black club when we're bad—like if we're really bad we get ten hits. He makes us pull down our pants, so we can feel it, so we know we've been bad." His huge eyes are larger and wider than a two-year-old's and don't catch a tear, but mine almost do.

My heart is shattered. I don't know what to say. He is so tiny, scarcely making it to my hip when he stands straight.

"He hits you?" I barely whisper.

"Only when we're bad. It all depends on how bad we are. You get one or two if it's not so bad, and three, four and five when you do something bad. And really bad, you get more."

I have no idea what to say. "How does that make your heart feel?" I'm looking for an emotional response, but instead he says, "It really hurts, it really hurts. That's why he makes us pull down our pants."

"Really?" I say softly.

"Yeah. What do you do if your kids are bad?"

"Zach, well, just to let you know, we don't do that here."

"What do you do?"

"Well, we talk about it and give you the choice to do it differently."

"What about time-outs?" he asks. That's when Alex comes into the garage from outside, wondering where we all are and says, "Oh yeah, I used to get time-outs all the time—but my parents took this class and now we talk and talk. Come on, let's go biking."

Zach walks out to the driveway where Alex has the bikes set up, but Zach isn't interested in biking; after all, this is only his second playdate all year, his second chance to be with another kids' parents, and he wants to talk—talk it all out. So he explains to Alex what the black club is and that it's made out of wood and where it lives in their house and what you have to do in order to have it slapped so hard on your butt that it makes you cry and sometimes you can't breathe even if you get one hit and it's hard to walk afterward.

Alex doesn't know what to do with this information, doesn't know how to process something so foreign. So when

215

he sees that Zach has finished speaking, he leads him to a bike and they ride in the cul-de-sac in front of our house with helmets on, bodies protected. Protected for now, or at least for this playdate.

I am still sitting on the garage floor, well after I have put on the helmet for Cole, stunned and overwhelmed. I watch them as if in slow motion as they ride in circles.

When it is time to take Zach home after the boys have played, been fed, laughed, rolled around on the grass, and started to get tired, I put all three in the car and go. Zach's father isn't home when we arrive, but Rosa is there; I wish I spoke better Spanish, but it wouldn't matter because I wouldn't know what to say. But I look at her, I mean I really look at her, and wonder if she knows what I know. But when she feels the intensity of my stare she looks away, says *Gracias,* and closes the door to their home.

CHAPTER
Thirty-Seven

*"Anger must come from judgment. Judgment is
the weapon I would use against myself,
to keep the miracle away from me."*

Katie, Jack, and the kids are coming over for dinner. Jack is back in the weave of work and family—a new normal. His hair isn't the only thing that grew back; he's on the road to recovery—moving slowly and magnificently. It wasn't his body that was healing so much as his soul, like a second chance at life—his own rebirth. He let go of the things that he held to so tightly—his pain. He jumped into his life and saw the beauty in his physical breakdown.

They come down early so the kids can play and we can sip on cocktails. We are going to grill, and Katie brought down one of her best salads. I made a pie—apple, country-style, not with an uptight crust edge, but loose and relaxed, with syrupy apple goo coming out of the sugary slots on top.

The temperature is in the seventies, the sky is blue, and

the sun is shining as it should at three in the afternoon. We carefully examine Jack when he walks through the door, as if to gauge how fragile he is. He feels at a disadvantage, even though he knows us and knows that we love him. But he isn't fragile—he seems strong.

Without words, Blake embraces him, a brotherly hug, perfectly silent, and when he pulls back he warmly asks, "How about a beer?"

"Sounds good."

The decibels of sound stay low for only a second; the kids screech and yell when they see each other.

It's when the meat is on the grill, giving off that barbeque smell into the air, that the conversation goes from casual to real. Men and grilling mix like cavemen and fire—naturally.

"How you doing, buddy?" I overhear Blake ask as I approach them, bringing out marinated vegetables. Then I stop, because I don't want them to see me and stop talking.

"Better than I thought I was capable of."

Blake nods and looks at him like he understands everything, as if it had happened to him, and then he grabs Jack's shoulder like guys do, and rubs it and kind of pulls him towards him. It's as if he's saying, *I'm here, buddy; I'm here and it's okay. You're alive and we all love you, and you're okay now.*

Men have a shorthand that women don't always have, this foreign but real body language that speaks volumes—that says the things that they are incapable of saying. I barely make out *Nonne amicus cerus in re incerta cernitur,* which later Blake translates as "A friend in need is a friend indeed." They talk as they grill, cooking the steaks, chicken, and hot dogs.

Inside the house, as we're setting tables and getting organized for dinner, I tell Katie the story about Zach. She is, surprisingly, not alarmed or in the same emotional conflict that I am—she's calm, too calm. Especially when she asks, "Well, does he hit them because he gets frustrated?"

"What? Who cares *why* he does it, he does it."

"Well, maybe that's how he was raised."

"What is wrong with you? That doesn't make it right."

"But maybe he doesn't know better."

"He's destroying his children—tearing the fiber of who they are. He's not only hurting them physically, he's crushing their souls."

"Don't you think you're overreacting?"

"No!" I say, like, *What is wrong with you?* I give her a look like she's turned into a pod-person.

"So what are you thinking of doing?" she says, tossing the salad.

"Scream up to the clouds and ask, 'Why is this happing to such a beautiful child?'"

"And then what?" She gives me a nonchalant look.

"I don't know. I'm still processing it all ... I ... I want to do something."

"Why? What happens if the father finds out?" she says, almost too quickly, as if she is jealous of a child who someone would want to save. After all, no one reached out and saved her when she was small and helpless. Still, I'm stunned by her resistance to fighting for what is right.

"I hope he does find out. Maybe he'll change."

"You wouldn't want him to come after you," she adds.

"I was thinking more along the lines of helping a helpless child. I can take care of myself. Maybe I should go to the school and get some advice. Or see if they've seen anything strange with Zach. If something horrible is actually happening, by law the school has to do something—right?"

"I guess, if you want to be killed in your sleep."

I look at her as if she has lost her mind. "You're kidding, right? You don't think I should even do that much?"

She changes the subject. "What do you think, should we have a separate table for the kids or make it all one?"

"One."

Dinner looks natural to the ordinary bystander. Blake and Jack make up stories for the kids in different accents as we eat; Jack is notorious for his pirate brogue and has everyone in hysterics. They're goofballs, more like brothers than forced friends—better friends than I think Katie and I are at that moment.

We did that, Katie and I; we forced them to be friends out of our own selfishness. But the truth is, they were born to be friends, we just put them together; but now I feel like I'm being forced to be friends with Katie.

After dinner Jack stands up and announces, *"Conlige suspectos semper habitos,"* or "Round up the usual suspects," and I know he's going to perform. He brought his guitar, a bit dusty and out of tune from months of neglect, and he sings, sings a song about family. And at that moment I wonder how Katie could do anything other than adore this man, and how she of all people could feel anything less than compassion for an innocent child.

CHAPTER
Thirty-Eight

"Let me remember I am one with God,
at one with all my brothers and my Self,
in everlasting holiness and peace."

My mother-in-law is like a Chihuahua—small, hyper, and yapping. She wears her hair like she has since college, as if she hasn't aged. A towhead-blond bob—blond from a bottle, stiff and brittle like her temperament. When she smiles it's tight and strained, like a bad face-lift.

My in-laws once gave me a description of their nephew's girlfriend—my mother-in-law's brother's son's girlfriend, that is. I had met the girlfriend, whose name was Bridgette, the summer after her second year of graduate school. She was attending Yale and had done undergrad at Harvard, where she graduated second in her class. To say she was brilliant was like asking, *Does the air have oxygen in it?* My in-laws described her as a nice girl, smart, brown hair, from Chicago. They said "smart" like they said everything else, like it was something that she was born with, something that you don't aspire to be or work hard to obtain.

It still baffles me. They view intelligence as something you either have or don't have. Genetic. Why do people pass off things that are hard to get, something that you have to push at, something that entails real work, as genetic? You either believe in God or you don't, it's genetic. If you're fat and can't lose weight, it must be genetic. If that person is smart, it's genetic. You either got it or you don't, end of story.

But now it's years later and I finally get it. They've never had any desire to be smarter or work harder or even be just plain caught up on things. They don't like to read and would never consider a crossword puzzle from a newspaper beyond the *Enquirer*. They're fine with being ill-informed. They act resigned to it, as if they were born with no other choice.

I understand how and where my husband gets his dysfunction. It hits you square in the face after being with his parents for more than three minutes. They're not bad people, just stuck. Happy-stuck. I-can't-and-won't-do-anything-about-it stuck.

It all came crashing down on my husband, just like it did on Jack. I don't mean that he got cancer; he got stuck in his own evolution—he had to deal with his own demons without someone to hold him up and support him. He had to deal with where he came from and what it did to him.

Here's the problem: I started to get my act together. I stopped calling him at 4:00 wondering when he was going to be home, would he be there to share dinner or to tuck the kids in. You see, when I starting taking better care of myself, I started to have more energy for the kids. If I wrote or worked on the books that day or did a second meditation, if I got a workout in, or a beach walk, or a yoga tape, that good feeling fueled me.

I realized when I depended on him to be home early or to help put the kids to bed, he would, almost invariably, be late. The more I wanted and needed him, the more he would push back. The sheer waiting on someone I couldn't control exhausted me. It was an opportunity to get worked up. So once I let it go, things fell into place—for me at least.

He wasn't so easily amused by the shift. I stopped picking up his dry cleaning, telling him, "Oh, honey, I'm so sorry, I just couldn't get to it. Maybe you could drop it off or have it picked up at work." He looked at me as if I had grown a second head, a look that I just ignored. There were fewer special meals for him too, which he didn't like either—no more of his beloved dinners that required exotic ingredients and took an hour to make.

My brain was now left for me rather than for his consumption, dietary or otherwise. I made the meals for me and the kids; that way, if he wasn't there when we ate, I didn't have to worry about it's not being good enough when he reheated it, or that it wasn't prepared exactly the way he wanted.

I stopped trying to please him with all the little things, and it started to add up. He'd have to make something on his own, do things for himself; after all, I was a working woman now. A working woman who got paid, that is—with money and respect. For a guy who cooked only two meals in the thirteen years we were together, that was a tough thing to swallow, even though it made my life easier.

I stopped playing the tug-of-war, because I wasn't even pulling. He didn't know what to think about it at first, and I'm not saying I didn't feel guilty. But once I got over that I felt liberated. More energy for me, less for him—I was invincible. He, however, was not so delighted.

So he became the master of making grilled cheese sandwiches, cereal, and overcooked eggs for dinner. He was now his own Cordon Bleu chef—the angry chef. Because his misery was not supported, he had a lot to discuss at therapy, and there he began to spin and spin and whine. I began to see things clearly; I began to see why women leave their mates twice as often as men leave theirs. I just let him spin on his gerbil wheel while I observed, observed him and me and wondered why it took me so long to do this.

Like finding a warm spot when swimming in a lake, I had found comfort in my own search for a better reality. Blake was still treading in cold water.

The phone rings and it's Katie. "Hey, what's up?"

And just when thought I lost the connection with her, she comes shining through. The day before, our discussion about Zach had made me question both our friendship and her sanity, and now I realized I could still love her for all her flaws. She was the same as me—needing advice and needing to sound off, too. Her voice is edgy when she asks, "Why don't men want to solve marital problems?"

"Because they don't think anything is wrong." I am in my office when I say this.

"Why do we have to be the major force for resolving conflict? And why is it when we give up, the marriage is over?" I am stunned that this is coming from her.

"Men think that our problems, or what we see as our problems, are something beyond them. If there's something wrong with the marriage, it's out of reach, too big, too complex for them to handle. They freeze and do nothing. Well, they do nothing but have sex, because it comforts them, and then they think everything is better because sex is a doorstep down from God."

She laughs.

I continue, "Yeah. Washing the cars on the weekend is a big deal, it's their way of writing a poem. Taking out the garbage before they go to the office, maybe reading a book to the kids at bedtime, bringing home the paycheck ... that's all they can handle. They're linear. They can do only so many tasks—tying their shoes and talking on the phone at the same time is Cirque de Soleil to them."

"Yeah, I get it," she says.

"If you ask them to improve the way they raise their children or to increase their financial support, it puts them over the edge. They become emotionally exhausted, because they have hit their max. They feel like all they get is criticism and no support, which drains them to the point where they close down."

"Okay," she says, taking in my words.

I have some metaphysical music on and it sounds like pixie dust. A perfect backdrop to my momentary status as a prophet. I feel as if I have added a grain of help to Katie's endless beach of wisdom. I watch the shadows of the palm tree sway back and forth, the light flickering through.

I am on a roll. She asks if I got all this information from an article. My insecurity hears this as, *There's no way this can be a personal observation, it sounds too logical to have come from you.* But then again, maybe not.

I continue, "Our husbands' roles have become more complex than their fathers'; they are in delivery rooms, they change diapers now, they drive the kids to school. Modern men think that women are impossible to please, that we're born to complain and that they must ignore it in order to survive. The reason women file for divorce more than men is this: women feel neglected by their men when they close down, when they can't or won't communicate, when they act indifferent. No matter what men say, even if it is well intended, they're shut down. They are inadvertently driving the women crazy, and the women label their men "mentally cruel"—the guys don't have a chance. Neglect is why women want to leave—no approval, no acknowledgment—but how plugged in are we to them?"

"Nah," she dismisses, not wanting to believe me even though she knows there is some truth.

"Huh?"

I take a deep breath and see from my open office door the altar on the fireplace mantel in the living room. This spot is where six candles are lit among pictures of the Madonna and baby Jesus and two rosaries, and there are chunks of bright crystals and a slab of amethyst. There is a small carved wooden Buddha that could fit in the palm of your hand. The Buddha holds a marble tray, and that is where I place the incense that burns and is given up to God as an offering to say, *Remember me? I still need you.* I clear my throat. "That's not the root—" I walk around the house with the cordless 'til I get to our bedroom, the room with the best view of the mountains miles away.

"You got to get to the root—neglect comes from lack of connection, spiritual connection. When the connection is gone, the marriage gets wobbly and then finally crumbles and dies. We're different animals—we see things differently, we do things differently, we are different, but once we are connected by the soul and spirit, the differences are embraced and we balance each other. And when we realize we balance each other, we pick up where the other cannot; we become more simpatico when we are spiritually one. Keep the spiritual connection alive and all is well. Once we're connected, we bring the other into our life."

"This doesn't sound like you. Are you reading a script?"

"I'm trying it on for size, and practicing it on you. I have felt glimmers of love, real love, because I want to get the connection back in my own marriage. Something has shifted in me and I want to do a better job with Blake."

"I think it's a bunch of crap."

"I think what I have to do is look into his eyes, and I mean really look, touch him like I did when we first dated, go to bed with a teddy on instead of the old granny jammies. I think I want to hold on; I don't want this to slip through my fingers. But love is funny—it can surprise you even if you only believe a little in it, as long as you just let a trickle in. It makes its way in and spreads like magic and then all of a sudden I remember how I first fell in love with him."

"You sound pathetic."

"Yeah, so—" I say.

"Gotta go," she says as I hear her kids arguing in the background.

I hang up the phone; it's Saturday. The boys are in the back playing putt-putt with real putters and real golf balls and a makeshift course made out of a SpongeBob cup and a collection of sippy cups without the lids.

The phone rings only seconds after I have hung up with Katie. It's my mother-in-law.

"Hello Tate. Is Blake there?" My mother-in-law's voice is more frazzled than usual.

"Hey, Katherine. I'll get him." Blake takes the phone in the kitchen. "Hi Mom," he says with no emotion. "...Uh, huh ...Uhm." His face becomes serious, the space between his eyebrows so tight it looks painful. "... Mmnh ... When? ... What did they say?"

The kids are in the kitchen making too much noise, so Blake has to put a finger in his ear to hold them out and her

in. "How long? Should I come out? Okay …Yeah, alright."
I give the kids a bottle of bubbles from the cabinet of special toys and shoo them outside.

"What?" I ask as he gets off the phone.

"Dad's in the hospital. They think it's pancreatic cancer.
They operate on Monday and he starts chemo in a couple
of weeks." Pancreatic cancer. That explains his dad's jaun-
diced appearance and sudden weight loss.

Blake is flushed; I go over to give him a hug, and he
walks away.

"Honey, I'm so sorry. How are they?"

He's stuck. He wants to tell me but doesn't want to be
nice to me because he's still in a withholding pattern—a
place of resolute stubbornness. If I weren't stable or secure
in myself in this moment, I could take it as meanness, or
simply being an asshole. But I get it. He doesn't want to
go to Pennsylvania but feels a moral obligation. He doesn't
want to deal with his dad in the hospital; after all, they don't
serve drinks there, and his dad will be miserable, demand-
ing painkillers.

Blake doesn't want to see his number-one demon in that
state, a vulnerable state, a state that might demand forgiveness, complete forgiveness.

The kids have come back into the kitchen. Cole is
slouched with his arms across his chest and his lower lip
sticking out beyond his chubby cheeks. "Don't go Daddy.
Please stay."

Blake pushes his fingers through his hair before he
speaks, as if it takes great pains to deliver his thoughts. He
casts his eyes to the side of my face, not making eye contact,
and says, "I think I should go."

And so he goes, and I'm glad that he's big enough to
do the right thing. I hope and pray for an epiphany, for

something grand and great that will soften his heart and let miracles happen. Something on the level that allowed Jack to deal with the ordeal of cancer or whatever they were calling it. But no such luck—Blake is slow moving when he isn't running, running away from his own fears.

CHAPTER

Thirty-Nine

"Let miracles replace all grievances."

All the Oprah and Dr. Phil and AA had done wonders for the couple, for the couple called my in-laws—they seem to have made an actual difference. With all the shows on how to be a better parent, they saw that their hitting, spanking, using a belt, verbal abuse, and the host of other nightmares associated with alcoholism—the alcoholism of Blake's dad, that is—weren't the best tools for raising their children. So they attempted to apologize. The cancer, of course, had something to do with it too.

But Blake wasn't ready to confront it, to forgive them, because that would mean accepting that it really did happen, that the past he wanted to forget really had existed.

His dad says, "We make mistakes, but we strive to do what's right."

Blake doesn't answer.

"All right then," his father says, heaving himself off the

sofa that had become his home away from his new hospital home. He staggers as he moves, wobbly and weak. He heads to the kitchen for something. Anything. Something and anything that will prohibit him from letting a tear roll down his cheek. Blake stays behind in the floral wingback chair, stoic and stubborn, neither flinching nor acknowledging.

Well done, he thinks to himself. *Or was it?*

He doesn't know the fate of his dad's cancer, that it may be the last time to get it right with him. To forgive him, to forgive him completely so that the past could be released and real living could start. His dad's efforts to reach out are too much for Blake, even though it would have been the best medicine. But sometimes the best medicine is hard to swallow.

Forty

"I can be free of suffering today."

There was a time when my in-laws could get under my skin, but all that has become undone. I used to fear they would repeat the pattern that they started with their own children and finish with mine—hitting and spanking. So I watched them like a hawk, but to my surprise they seem to have gone the other way—overcompensating for their mistakes. I guess grandkids can do that—they give you a second chance.

I am never thrilled when they come to visit, but it's never as bad as I think it will be either. As long as they weren't sharing their political views or thoughts on world affairs, I could tolerate them. And my in-laws were good with little kids. They knew that children weren't made of rubber, so they watched them carefully, almost too carefully. They feared the worst, but the upside was the kids would never get a bruise, scrape, bump, or a hair out of place in their presence.

The kids loved them for the close attention and the toys. My in-laws were big on toys— and they would bring a bunch despite my insisting that they not. "It's a grandparent's job to spoil their grandchildren," they would say.

No damage done.

They came to visit after Blake Sr.'s operation and chemo. Chemo is a common theme, another thing my in-laws share with the Welk family; both women also share the same name. Katie, my best friend, and Katherine, my mother-in-law—polar opposites. I wonder what God's intention was in creating two women so profoundly different but with the same name—probably just God's twisted sense of humor.

Katherine, with her good Belgian roots, likes to have things clean, like her son. When things didn't feel right or weren't going well in her life, she cleaned. You could look at it as a need or want to control or as OCD depending on her mood.

What didn't feel right for both Katherine and Blake Sr. was the lack of a liquor cabinet. Sure they could drink in our house, but we knew the doctor's orders and Blake Sr.'s strict diet—fat and alcohol the missing ingredients. But it wasn't just about the lack of alcohol, it was also the lack of communication—Blake's and his father's.

The tension became thick when my husband puttered furiously and feverishly around the house. His nervous energy didn't bother me, but Katherine picked up on his edgy movements and tried to help him by cleaning the kitchen counters, which already shone like freshly polished mirrors.

Blake Sr. was watching *Blues Clues* with the kids when my husband came in to fetch scissors from the kitchen drawer. "Hey buddy, can I help you outside?"

"I got it, Dad," was his too-curt answer. Any dummy

could see that Blake Sr. was hurt, so Cole, being his typical empathetic self, sat in his grandpa's lap.

I slowly followed my husband out to the backyard, and when no one could hear me I whispered, "Why don't you take your dad out to the range and hit a bucket of balls?"

"Tate, there's a lot that needs to be done around the house." *Yikes*, he had his snarl face on, and I crept back slowly so that I wouldn't get stricken by his venom. With a limp hand up and face slightly bowed, I muttered, "Just a suggestion—"

He grumbled as I walked back into the kitchen.

"What do you all feel like for dinner tonight? You want to go out?" I asked the kids and grandparents, who were still sitting in the family room.

That's when Blake came in. "Tate, we're staying in and grilling. Do you have to try to control everything?!" And then the repeat sneer, like, *What is wrong with you? Can't you see I have this all under control?* I took a deep breathe because it hurt. It hurt my feelings and I didn't want it to.

I was waiting for anyone to take my side of the argument, I mean agree with me. But not even one taker. Fighting the tickle in the back of my throat, I silently vowed never to try to help him out again, a vow that would be broken in half an hour.

When dinner did come, the lights were dimmed so low, you could barely see the silverware. No one said anything, even though we had to eat with our faces inches from our food. I dared not turn up the light for fear of losing a limb.

My marinade on the chicken was perfect, giving the meat flavor and tenderness that melted in your mouth, not to mention the salad—another recipe from Katie, of course. *Uhms* and *Ahs* came from my in-laws. There was a shrug and a small nod of acknowledgment from Blake—a very small nod of acknowledgment, probably the quota for the day.

Wow! Yipee! I exist.

The table was cleared, the kids had their baths, books were read, and shortly thereafter, the grandparents went to bed. Blake found me in the kitchen making a cup of tea. The microwave buzzed and I opened it to take my mug out when Blake said, "Thanks, Tate."

"Huh?" I said, looking at him. His eyes were cast down and his body was soft.

"Thanks. I know it's tough having them here." He leaned against the island in the center of the kitchen and looked straight at me.

I went over and gently hugged him; his shoulders yielded and he hugged me back. I whispered in his ear, "It's fine ... I get it—I really get it." I pulled my body apart from his and gave him a look like, *Don't worry, it's all going to be okay.*

"I know you do," he said with a warm smile, and added, "I couldn't get through it without you."

His love washed over me from out of the blue and reminded me why I married him. But more importantly, it reminded me that it's okay to hold on even when times are hard.

The thing about Blake is this: Even though it didn't look like he was changing and evolving—he was. Maybe not as fast as I had hoped, or as fast as his parents hoped either, but it was happening. Evolution can't always be seen from the outside, because it's all about what's happening on the inside.

CHAPTER

Forty-One

"God's answer is some form of peace. All pain
is healed; all misery replaced with joy.
All prison doors are opened. And all
sin is understood as merely a mistake."

Katie dropped off five paintings at a gallery in down-town San Diego and came over right after to show me some illustrations. We're sitting in the heart of my home, the kitchen. The coffee has been ground and smells bold and strong through the French press. Sweetened powdered cocoa was sprinkled on top of each cup before the milk was poured in—perfection. It was served in green milk-glass cups with matching saucers, the same color as the porcelain cake stand that holds the store-bought peach torte.

Outside we spot a lizard the size and width of my thumb—it's scurrying across the patio pavers and then sud-denly stops in a sunny spot. It doesn't flinch or move, as if it's set in stone, then it does push-ups, trying either to make

236

itself bigger or to catch a peek of something that may be in front of him. It is so cute that we both laugh.

I've finished my first cup of strong coffee. The buzz sets in, putting me in a good mood, maybe even a little hyper and chatty, where I feel like I can do anything, like run a marathon. So I decide to have a second cup, which makes my chatter too loud—the type of loudness that makes people back away a little, as if you have bad breath.

"Give me your observations," Katie says after one sip.

"The more I meditate, the more I feel guided to well-being."

"Be specific."

"When I close my eyes and quiet my mind to a moment of stillness, I feel like I'm letting in who I really am—letting in some type of Source energy that you could call God. Once I allow myself to feel connected to God's energy and love, I feel appreciated and loved, enthusiastic and passionate. When I don't meditate, I feel frustrated, uneasy, angry—depressed and in fear—and I can't feel God's guidance. It's as if I've closed off the valve and then everything else closes off, like my kids and husband. When I let my husband in like I let God in, the details are taken care of, like calling a babysitter on date night."

"Yep, you're dreaming. Married men are not capable of getting a babysitter unless they're doing them."

I am surprised that my woo-woo comments on meditation are not tangible for her. But I understand how she feels; I'm always cutting off my valve to Source.

So I go to her space by saying, "No kidding—men. They think a shower and a smile is all they have to do—like their fresh scent will drive us crazy. For them all we have to do is show up naked with food. They have no idea what we need from them—it's definitely not a naked man with a bowl of fruit."

Katie changes the subject. "I feel so out of touch with what's current. There used to be a time when I could ask someone, 'Who's worth listening to? What's hot in the music scene?'"

"That was before kids, when we had time to waste," I say.

I take the last sip of coffee and look over the rim to her. "I saw Zach's father at drop-off a week ago." She knows I am talking about Zach and the club.

"Yeah?" Her face has turned red, her eyes dilate.

I look outside the window because I don't want to look at her face. It will make me more uncomfortable than I already am. However, I think she loves that little child as much as I do, and she knows the harsh reality of it all. "And I felt like I wanted to talk to him even though my stomach was in knots."

She says nothing.

"But it wasn't the time or place, so I didn't."

She pretends to be relieved but I know she is not.

I continue, "I've watched his kids at school. They're so quiet, so polite. Their eyes are so wide, like they're caught in the high beams of a car."

My gaze goes to her cheeks, which are still flushed like she's just stolen a barrette from a drugstore. She says nothing. And then I spill the beans.

"But two days later it was different. He was walking to his car and I was walking in alone. No one was around, so I asked him if he had a minute."

"You didn't," she almost whispers.

"He said he did. So, I told him that we enjoyed having Zach over but there was something that Zach said that bothered me." I didn't give Katie all the details, she couldn't have stomached it. I didn't tell her that I touched his sleeve gently when I said, "I know that parenting is hard and rais-ing kids can be overwhelming." I didn't tell her how I ex-tended my heart to this man instead of blaming him for how he raised his children. I just gave her the *CliffsNotes*. "You were right. He was very defensive, but I let him know that I understood and told him that I was raised that way too. I lied, but I felt I could because it was the way Blake was raised."

She says nothing.

"I told him that I had learned a lot from my Redirect-ing Children's Behavior classes. And I wasn't preachy but I made my point. He walked away mad after we talked, but not the mad like he was going to hit his kids or kill me in my sleep. It was the embarrassed kind of mad."

"And—"

"Yesterday, I ran into him again and he thanked me. He said he was going to check out the classes and that he didn't want to repeat what was done to him anymore." I didn't tell her that he looked into my eyes when he said it, like he meant it.

I look at Katie, and she's frozen in time. Now I look straight into her eyes like a dart to the bullseye. And I don't flinch and I don't let up and I am not going to let it go. We are talking about this—this delicate matter that she won't talk about, ever.

She snaps out of it. "Well, I think you're stupid for doing that."

"I don't. I think I did something right—I followed my gut. His kids got a second chance."

"Well, how would you have liked it if some stranger said something to your dad when you were a kid? Something like, 'Stop yelling at your kids.'"

I laugh at how ridiculous her analogy is. "I would have

thought, *Okay, so this guy sees what I see, so I'm not the only one who sees this and maybe it isn't right for a father to rage at his kids,* and I would have thought, *Maybe he'll stop doing it, maybe he'll change.* I would have welcomed it even though it would never happen because he never yelled at us in public. And you?"

"And me what?"

"And how would you have felt?"

"I don't know what you're getting at."

"Just say it," I say, looking back outside.

"Say what?"

Now she has her chance at being real and looking at her demons like she asks me to do all the time. Now she has a chance to practice what she preaches. In a hint of a voice, I say, "Just say it and you will be free."

But she doesn't say it. She doesn't say a word about the past that scares her and torches her mind and soul. She looks far away from me. This dark ugly secret that propelled her to self-help. She resists this opportunity to look at her pain, exposed by chance because a small child came over to my house to play.

She gets up from the kitchen table and grabs a glass of water, takes a sip, and says from the kitchen sink, "I know what you're thinking, but this is so much different. This has nothing to do with me."

"Whatever." I'm done trying—done trying to draw it out of her. *Go ahead,* I think, *Go ahead and feel helpless, like you did as a child; go ahead, repeat the pattern.* She reads my mind.

"You know I did the best I could."

"I know," I say calmly.

"I was only a small child."

"I know you were."

240

She grips the water glass like she could crush it in her small palm. "But then why couldn't I have helped her?" she says like it happened yesterday, and her eyes fill with tears. I walk over to her and stretch my hands towards and around her shoulders.

"Why couldn't I have just spoken up and said something?" She is talking about her older sister, who was awakened in the middle of the night by her father to have sex—to be raped.

Her older sister Anne was eleven and Katie was eight. Katie knew it happened because she walked in one night from a bad dream only to see a more terrible nightmare. Frozen in time, frozen stiff, she never mentioned it to Anne or her mother. Her mother found out a few years later, just in time to save Katie from the abuse. But the damage was done; Anne's body and spirit were ripped in half and never healed.

The secret lay dormant in their family, until the divorce came. It was a family that outsiders said could have survived anything. But they didn't know the things that brought them there, how deep and wide the wounds were and that they could never form a scab to fully heal.

In this moment she wants to heal from the anxiety of it all, so I take the tools that she has given me over the years. I ask her to be with her thoughts, so that I can help her to work through all that is stuck in her subconscious, to release the feelings that lay dormant below her nerves. And after she purges out the words that hold her posture in tight, she begins to go through the memories of her lurid past. I coach her to forgive herself and to let go. Her shoulders go from stiff and knotted to relaxed and yielding.

And now the next layer of the onion—we talk from past to present. I open up the can of worms when I ask, "Are you having an affair with the gallery guy?"

"No!" in a tone that says, *Give me a break.*

"Did you?"

"No." But her voice is not as strong.

"Did you want to?"

"Tate. Really!"

"Really what?"

"God, you don't let up, do you? Okay, so I flirted with the guy and yes, it could have moved in that direction. But I stopped it. I know you are not going to believe it, but he helped me give Jack a second chance."

"I don't get it."

"One month ago we started to see a family counselor."

Finally, I think. "Why didn't you tell me?"

She ignores my question and says, "We both felt the distance ... I thought we could figure it out on our own. I thought I could live my life without him, but maybe not."

"You're right; I don't believe you."

"Tate, things don't always fit in a perfect package. Life is messy and complicated. You of all people should be happy. We're taking a stab at making it work."

"I know, I know. You're right." The room turns to silence and she walks to the kitchen sink and cleans off the dirty plates covered with crumbs. *I am so glad she is my friend.*

She turns around and asks, "Did I ever tell you what my grandmother said to me before she died?"

"The grandma that lived in Spain?"

"Yeah. She was talking about the lessons she had learned about life and legacy. It was an old Spanish saying."

Her eyes go down to the floor as if she's picking up the words from the ground. "It was simple. 'Before you die you must plant a tree, have a child, and write a book.'"

We are eye to eye; the weight of the room seems light as

we look at each other, like two stone columns, absolutely still.

"Let's go plant a tree," she says.

"Okay."

Katie beams, "No, seriously. Let's."

CHAPTER
Forty-Two

"Above all else I want to see things differently."

The grocery list of all the things we are missing is in my head: paper towels, butter, apples, olive oil, and I think I'd better write these down before it's too late and I forget them. But I don't write them down because I've got to get dinner started and keep to the schedule that runs the family so well, or so I think.

"Hey, Mom, come check out this spider," says Alex from the backyard, his little brother crouched beside him as if they have just discovered gold. They are squatted like elders from a tribe in the Yucatan.

"In a minute," I say as I pull things out of the pantry. I stop at the refrigerator, and after everything is laid on the counter I am about to run downstairs to the load of laundry that needs to go in the dryer or it will go musty and then stink. And then something goes off in my brain—*this is that moment.* It is as if God bonks me with a pillow in my face, not hard but not soft either. This is that moment where I am supposed to *Drop and Go*—Drop what I am doing, and Go see the spider. This is that moment that I have to let dinner go a little later, even if it means the boys will be hungry and might get whiny and cranky.

This is the moment where I have to forego that musty smell that is settling into the sheets, because if I don't I'll lose it and never get it back. And I'll be old and in that rocker regretting, regretting that I didn't savor and slow down for my children when they were small and precious, and I would hear myself saying that thing that I hate hearing: "They grow up so fast—treasure it."

And so I walk toward them and take a breath and crouch down like a mother tiger next to her cubs. And I look at this spider that, if I weren't wise enough, would make me screech—or better yet, want to step on it—versus admire its legs and bulbous body with my boys who are in such awe.

I feel so much better that I did come out to look at it, and I know I can go to bed and think, *Okay, I got that moment right.*

The dinner is made and the boys are almost done when Blake comes home grumpy and tired, like me, but the difference is I hold it together and he can't. There are too many moving parts to getting the kids tucked in bed—the baths and then the relentless reminders to brush their teeth, to stop the horsing around, to get into jammies, to pick up scattered toys. Finally there's the book and the tuck-in. It's only when they are asleep that I can relax, and that moment feels like an eternity away.

It's a tiring and a frustrating process. The kids horse around and don't listen, and the infamous feeling of not being heard creeps into my bones and could start to rot. But the difference is that I know that it is part of life and I choose not to take it personally.

Blake moves slowly and barks orders in a nasty tone

and the kids are crying because they are too tired to accept it when he says that *there will be no stories tonight and I mean it.* I try to go into their rooms and rub their backs to let them know it's okay and that they are really loved even though they don't believe it, but Blake says, "Don't go in there! They've had enough."

So I wait until he's not around and I sneak them a kiss, but that just gets them wound up, because they want more, and I am busted, because now Blake hears them.

"Tate! I said don't go in there!"

I tiptoe to the bathroom to get away from him and let him have his space and eat the dinner I made. Then, when the time comes, when I think that he has unwound and begun to relax, I go down to the kitchen where he is eating herb chicken with rice and not a grilled cheese sandwich that he had to make himself. I try to connect to him and let him know I love him and care. "Hey, so how was your day?"

"Fine."

"Anything good happen?" I say with a smile, searching for his eyes to see mine.

"Do we have to talk about it?" he says, flinching away from me.

"Nope, just asking."

So I reach for a mug and add water to make tea and I think, *Another night—of this.* I let out a slow breath and quietly sit next to him at the table and wait—wait for a miracle.

And then when I have had enough of waiting I begin, "I just want to be your friend. I just want to know that you love me sometimes—and maybe adore me a little and that things will be okay."

"And what about me? Do you adore me?" His eyes are downcast and mean.

And in that moment I don't, but I decide to lie. "Yes."

But he's too smart or still too grumpy to believe a lie and says, "Well, you sure have a strange way of showing it." And I want to say, *Oh really, and you're so easy to adore?* But I don't, because I'm tired of arguing and picking on and hating him when he is really just tired. So I say nothing. I say nothing and hope to God that this tug-of-war game that we play will stop once and for all. And I take a deep breath and let out the air, which comes out too loudly, so loudly that he hears my frustration and rolls his eyes.

He says nothing, and this is the moment I should *let it go and not take him personally,* but I do—the slow learner that I am. Finally, after what seems like the longest time, like looking back to prehistoric life, I say, "Blake, I'm trying, I'm really trying, and I'll try harder because, yes, I do love you. I really do." And this time I mean it and this time he knows and he looks up from his dinner and his eyes are beginning to soften and I try to look for that piece that makes him small, just like my boys.

But he's not ready to soften—not completely. He's not ready to relax into my trying.

"I really want us to love each other," I say. And now I feel like I will start crying because I mean it and want it so badly that I could just break in half.

He sees my watery eyes and it looks like he is about to say something, but ultimately he says nothing. He lets out a slow breath and then offers a "Whatever."

In that moment, if I say one more thing, it will be the wrong thing. This is the crucial moment where you say nothing, where you let the ball bounce in his court and see if he picks it up.

"I guess I don't believe you," he says.

I could be defensive here, I could be all over him and let

him know exactly what I think of him, but then we would be in that space that we can never get out of. I want to get out of that kitchen so fast, but I don't. I take another breath and say, "Well, maybe one day you will." And I smile even though my heart hurts. I walk away after lightly touching his shoulders and I hope and I pray that all good things do come to those who wait if you have the right intentions.

Forty-Three

"I will be still an instant and go home."

Katie calls, high on something. She calls up to tell me, "We gotta get out of here!"

"Huh? What d'you mean?" I say while folding laundry, the phone wedged tightly into my collarbone.

"No husbands, no kids—a spa, a retreat, a getaway. That's what we need."

"Sounds good, but there's no way—"

"Why?" she says like a little girl, but not meaning to.

"Who's gonna look after the kids?"

"Our husbands."

"Yeah, right." She must be on crack.

"No, I'm serious. When was the last time you were away from your kids?"

"Never," I say, walking to put the folded laundry away.

"That's the problem. We're doing it, go tell Blake today. I'll find the spa—we'll go for just five days."

Maybe it's diet pills or something; she's speaking too fast.

"You're kidding, right?"

"Tate! I mean it, talk to him tonight—we're going within thirty days. Pack your bags."

"There is no way Blake is going to go for that."

"Don't give him an option; stand your ground. Don't worry, we'll line up the reinforcements—get the kids' schedules in order, maybe line up a babysitter for backup. You never know; we might need to send in the training wheels."

"Training wheels?"

"You know, the in-laws."

But Blake would do better without them.

She goes on, "This will be great for them. The kids need to see their dad in action, and they all need to be less dependent on you. Don't worry—just stand your ground!"

"But—" It was too late, she was gone—gone crazy over this ridiculous mission.

Yeah right, spa. Who was she kidding? There was no way Blake would buy into this nonsense, but I had to ask him. If I didn't, Katie would.

So there I was after the kids were tucked in bed and he had some time to really unwind, some quality downtime in the backyard. I tried to sound casual when I tossed out, "Hey, Katie and I are thinking of going away together on a retreat spa thing," but my face and my voice probably showed that I was prepared for the quick shutdown. Instead all I got was silence, so much silence that I was about to ask if he had heard me when he raised his eyes and looked directly at me. "That sounds great; you could use a break."

"Wha … what?" I thought I would have to come up with a list of reasons and excuses to defend my position. I thought I'd have to … I thought I would have to do something, and, yes, sexual favors were on the working template.

Then he added, "I didn't think you were really ready for something like this. The boys and I will be fine; you should go."

"Can we afford this?"

"Tate, it's okay—you should go."

And just like that, we had done the unthinkable; we thought of me first and it was as if time stood still and revealed the poetry of God and his angels.

And who said miracles don't happen.

There wasn't even a tradeoff. Blake asked for a weekend off too, which was more like a bonus, because when he was back he was so much easier to be around, and when he was gone, they boys and I could be on autopilot—mac and cheese every night.

Katie and I flew to Iowa and were picked up by a fancy car. Once inside, I leaned into Katie's shoulder and asked her, "Are they going to give us potato snacks too?"

"That's Idaho, silly. Would you just trust me on this."

And when we set foot in the grand lobby after walking through verdant, plush grounds, I did trust her, because this place was more beautiful than I could ever have imagined—this place was head and shoulders above any hotel I'd stayed in because of its intimacy.

The spa was surrounded by breathtaking mountains and decorated in the European country motif of the finest everything—custom furniture, tasteful honed marble flooring, dynamic fountains. The service was quietly over-the-top; each guest was made to feel as if he or she were there alone.

My bag was taken before I could set it down, and there was no check-in because they knew who we were and where we were to go. The tears just came rolling down. I realized Blake was in on the whole thing when I walked into our room where there were three bouquets of flowers—one each from him and my sons.

"You gotta be kidding. This is insane!"

"You ain't seen nothing yet!" We were there to escape, and I did—right out of my mind.

On the chaise lounge in the grand marble bathroom were clothes for my use while staying at the spa. Yes, that's right: all the clothes were in my size, and I don't mean just terry cloth robes, of which there were three—one for the bathroom, one for spa treatments, and a shorter, lighter one to lounge around in. I mean there was sportswear—shorts, shirts, polos, sweatpants, leisure pants, socks, flip-flops, monogrammed slippers, visors, hats, and sunglasses. These were quality clothes—nothing chintzy.

That's when I knew Blake had helped with the plans, because only he knows the sweats size I like, and then—feeling so guilty for judging him, when he had done something so wonderful for me—I began to cry again. The tears really flowed when I read the last card on the largest bouquet of flowers, which said, "Relax and don't call. Love, Your Boys."

The sounds of ocean and raindrops interlaced with space odyssey noises flowed from the portable player. The bed had at least a hundred pillows on it. There was a window seat with playful yellow and red damask pillows that looked inviting and comfortable, but you could tell no one actually sat on it. It was too perfect, like sculpture that you don't want to touch for fear of breaking it. If there were a cat or a dog on the premises, this would be the spot—out of the foot traffic and in a prime place for a sunbath. I was going to use that window seat before I went back home.

"Is this possible—is it possible to have something so grand and so good?" I ask Katie, who's biting into one of the pears from her room's fruit basket.

"Yep," she says, slurping up the juice and flesh of the

green and yellow fruit. "Come on, let's go check out the grounds." She was already in her polo shirt, sweatpants, and flip-flops.

I quickly changed and we ventured outside, taking in all the beauty. Everything was top of the line, from the clay tennis courts to the spa house done in imported blue and white European tiles—grand elegance. The gym was equipped with state-of-the-art machines, hand-crafted Pilates equipment, and free weights that were shiny and new. The walls were a muted stone color, with wall sconces that should live in Tuscany. Leather-tufted benches and silk-upholstered chairs that should have been in a fine living room were off to the side of each exercise room—just a place for a respite.

I just cried and cried.

"Is that how you're going to lose your water weight?"

"I feel so—human."

"Come again."

"I feel human—I forgot what it was like." The truth is, it wasn't the opulence that made me feel human; it just took getting away and having someone else serve the coffee, make my bed, fold my laundry, and look at me—I mean really look at me—and ask, *Is there anything I can get you?* and mean it. I had become whole after being cut into three pieces, not one belonging to me.

"Do you think we will have to give the trainers a note if we don't want to work out in the morning?"

"Nah. Just don't show and then give 'em one of Jack's favorites: *Canis meus id comedit.*"

I look at her like, *Translation please.*

"My dog ate it."

Outside my bungalow window was a slope of stone boulders, with moss growing in between. On top, the branches of a white-flowering Japanese tree cascaded like a waterfall. There was an omnipresent layering effect; the wall that goes to your waist, and then shrubs that go to your knee, and then flowering plants in the front, like kids lined up in a school play with the smallest in front. A tiny stream ran like a waterfall to a pond in the center of the property, framed by smooth rocks. I could see my reflection in the waters; it let me see myself as intact and complete. And I made sure to carry that home.

Before I came to the spa, Blake and I saw our therapist. She never came out and said, "Okay, you're healed. I never have to see you again," but she did say, "We can take a break now." She couldn't tell us all the work was done, because we understood that healing was a continuous progression. But she saw that we could say things to each other with love instead of blame; that we no longer needed her to be our referee. She saw that all our data logs of acknowledgment had transformed into changed behavior—*trained* changed behavior, that is.

Healing is never fully done—it ebbs and flows into recovery and happiness. Blake and I chose happiness and chose to find it in each other and all around us. And we realized that our process of our evolution was just that, a process.

After five days of bliss, when I am back home rested, relaxed and feeling whole, I realize *Yes, it is possible to fall in love with your husband like the first time.* As if fourteen years haven't passed. It is possible to love and honor him like I thought I would when I said my vows, maybe because I had some space to really look at my relationship and see how kind and generous he is and that, when it's all said and done, he really does care.

CHAPTER
Forty-Four

"I give the miracles I have received."

Arriving back from the spa, refreshed and in love with our lives, we were greeted by husbands who had short tempers and felt squelched. They were happy we were back so they could be free again. They had gotten a taste—a taste of what we do—and they were grateful it was us doing it, not them. But grateful nevertheless.

Blake—I have gotten used to his tapping the toothbrush on the porcelain sink. It used to bother me, but when I realized that I do the same thing, I let the irritation go. Also, he will take a Q-tip and, before swirling it in his ear, it meets his tongue for a generous licking. He says it's so the cotton stays together for a perfect cleaning. If I didn't love him, that would be gross.

When Katie walked through her door, after being drowned in hugs and kisses from her kids, Jack came forward to claim her. She asked how it went and he tried to put his ego aside and respond, knowing she would not be able to translate this one, *"Nihil sine labore,"* the Latin phrase meaning "Nothing without work." She gave him a quizzical look, like, *What does that one mean?* He just gave her a kiss on the cheek and said everything was fine.

The boys had bonded while we were gone—not our kids, our husbands. They had hooked up for a barbeque to thump their chests and say, "See, no problem, we can cook and take care of the kids too." But we knew the truth—it was all an act. We know they felt overwhelmed by all the moving pieces and the ramifications if those pieces didn't fall together. We know that late nights and overtired kids and the whining of little boys missing their warm beds and blankies—the consequences of going off schedule—may have made them realize, *Maybe she has a point—maybe a schedule isn't a bad thing.*

Of course we never heard the details of all the things they finally understood with us gone. Maybe all the things we bitch about had a purpose. They couldn't give in that easily, but they could say, "Glad to have you back," and mean it. And they could walk away easily from the mounding laundry with a gait that said, *Thank God I never have to do that again.*

Our husbands matured in more ways than one in our absence. They realized that they could rely on one another, just like their wives do.

It wasn't too many weeks later when our husbands ditched us for their own getaway weekend, a weekend where they found their own center and where they could say things that they couldn't say to their wives.

Their y-chromosome retreat included fresh air, physical therapy, and fire—campfire. They didn't have a plan, just an idea to bring along their favorite equipment—mountain bikes, running shoes, and tents. Their only strategy was to pick a spot that we wouldn't know about, where we couldn't find them, couldn't track them down even if we were undercover agents on a mission.

When we asked for the location, all we got were grunts that suggested that not even Chinese water torture could get it out of them.

We knew the game that they were playing, so we asked again to fuel their fire; they shrugged their shoulders and pointed to the sky and then looked down to their matching compasses, as if they succeeded. And they won—they never did tell us where they were going, and they left feeling triumphant in their quest, clapping each other's shoulders as they approached their getaway car to a place where cell phones don't work.

We couldn't have cared less where they went, as long as they got out of our hair.

The boys had gone away together before. But that was before chemo and before kids and before midlife crises and before Blake's dad, who would die soon after they got home. Now this was a chance for them to get close and be real and have a time where they could get something out of the weekend deeper and grander than open space.

It was a chance for them to review their lives and talk about the things that are hard to talk about and be real comrades. A time to share real brotherly love and friendship. It was more than beating on their chests and announcing to the world that they were survivors; it would be a time to shed tears and comfort each other.

Yeah, right, that happened. Not. They got drunk and pissed in the woods. When they weren't drunk or scratching their crotches, they tore up rocky paths on their bikes in full competitive mode—it was all about who could ride faster and harder. There was no singing by the campfire and spilling their guts about their lives. The only gut-wrenching sounds that came from deep inside of them were good belches or dense farts—potent gas that would be labeled in a baritone voice as *Juu-see.*

Forty-Five

"All that I give is given to myself."

Without any announcement or warning, Jack was fully in remission.

I happened to be at the Welks' house when he lumbered through the door, briefcase in one hand, keys in the other. His hair, once gone completely, and then a sprouting tuft that didn't all grow in the right direction, had finally grown back. There was no hint of what he went through. He was no longer that thin and pale version of himself. He looked remarkable.

There was not a word.

He came right toward Katie and swallowed her up in a hug that I thought would crush, shatter and break her. Burying his face in her hair could not conceal the tears that ran down his cheeks.

He pulled her back so he could look at her when he said, "My doctor says I'm clean and I don't have to go back for a year." That's right, no more doctor visits for a year.

"Daddy!" Somehow the kids knew he was home, and they came running from their rooms. Their bodies all in one mass; a family hug, holding on so tightly to each other as if saying, *Please, please never get sick again.*

I patted his shoulder, gave him a smile that said *Welcome home,* and tiptoed out. Katie would call when she was ready.

In that moment, I knew a veil had been lifted from my eyes. Judgment takes different shapes and forms. I judged Katie for the way she supported him, or didn't support him, and for making the choices I thought I would never make. She had to let him go on his own healing journey, sometimes away from the people whom he loved, so that he could focus on himself. And I understood the strength it took to let him go to do that. All while she had to deal with her own mortality and immorality.

She let him be his own pillar, standing alone, as she figured out how to be her own. Did he know about the tiptoeing in the garden of sin? When they went to therapy, did they talk about it? Yes, they had gone to therapy to talk about the cancer. I had no idea if they talked about her wandering eye—wandering body, mind, and soul. Their pillars had stood so far apart, where once they were too close; maybe now there was just enough distance to hold their temple strong. I forgave her. I mean I forgave myself for the way in which I judged her, because I now understood why. Understood why we do the things we do.

That night, back home tucking in my kids, I wonder how my boys will be as fathers. As I snuggle Cole's favorite stuffed animal next to him, I wonder what he'll be like to his wife. Probably kind. I wonder whether my sons will gain insight from the example that I set. Will they participate as fathers and value their wives? Will my sons' wives take care of themselves first as they raise their children, making sure they have enough breath to breathe life into their family? Will I be the mother-in-law who gets on their nerves? Will I get to see my grandchildren grow? Will my children be better parents than I, or will they go against all the things I believe in?

I trust they will do their best, like me. Getting some parts right and some wrong. But one thing I know for sure is that their kids will be loved.